BLAKE

A. MICHELE HENDERSON

DEDICATION

I dedicate this book to Team Blake. I'd like to thank all my readers who requested that I pull her character out of the trilogy and allow her to stand alone. As many of you know she is the first character I created who is loosely based on myself. My hope is that I created a work that my great grandchildren will benefit from. I encourage everyone who will ever read an A. Michele Henderson novel to create something that will outlive you. Be well.

ACKNOWLEDGMENTS

Amid all the chaos and uncertainty in this world, I would like to acknowledge the Almighty God, for being my source and anchor. To my husband James for the friendship and love we've shared for the past 12 years, Happy 11th Wedding Anniversary! I celebrate you and what we've built together, I love you. To our son Joshua, momma loves you to the moon and back. Thank you for reminding me to always believe in myself. You're wise beyond your 6 years and 9 months. To my biggest cheerleader in such a chaotic year, my mother Denise, I love you. To my mom-in-love Flora for being paper bible saved, I love and appreciate you greatly. To my cousin Ella-Frances, you lit the match that has me at published book number 8; I love you more than words can say, you're my A1 from day 1. Happy 80th rotation around the sun! To my father VB Hawk for always wanting the best for me, I love you daddy. To my paternal grandmother Ardena, for being an awesome example of strength and class; I love you Nana. To my mentor Misa for being someone I can always talk to and share my good news with, thank you for pouring into my life in such a mighty way! To my sister LaKesha, we've been through the fire together but

I'm honored to call you friend. Thanks for not giving up on me, I love you. To our mentor Pastor Curtis Hairston Jr. for allowing me to use his last name to create and illustrate a strong, upper middle class, Black family. To my aunts, uncles, cousins and extended family, thanks for your support, I love you all! To my die hard, till the wheels fall off: readers, watchers and supporters, here is the book you asked for, I pray you enjoy the ride!

CONTENTS

1. The Last Straw   1
2. The Score   21
3. Contention   36
4. Self Care   56
5. The Storm   83
6. Passing the Baton   110
7. Perfect Love   127
8. New Life   133

DISCLAIMER

amichelehenderson.com

The storyline of this novel is a work of fiction and does not depict the lives of actual persons. Real life locations and pop culture icons are used for context and relatability. The author reserves the right to reference herself as a writing signature.

1

THE LAST STRAW

*I*t was 3am when Blake entered the Capital Suite at the MGM National Harbor with her children Ryan Jr, Rayne and Royce in tow. Her cousin Lexi had booked the suite in her own name and made the temporary residence comfortable for their arrival. As an award-winning interior decorator, Lexi made sure that the children had the same items they enjoyed at home. Her husband Paris waited in the car because the reality of Blake leaving her home was disturbing. Afterall, Ryan is his first cousin, as are Blake and Lexi but Paris knew better than to choose a side. The man of God was 10,000 feet in the air on his way back from a preaching engagement, yet his wife of 14 years, was fleeing out of their home. Blake and Ryan were hashtag marriage goals but everyone has a breaking point. The children were exhausted when they entered the bedroom. Already in their pajamas, they took off their coats and crawled into the king size bed and fell fast asleep. Lexi made Blake a cup of tea with honey pearls as she sat quietly on the couch. Disbelief could be seen on Blake's face as she struggled to make sense of her current predicament. Likewise, feeling the same sense of disbelief, Lexi was at a loss for words. She knew firsthand how tumultuous the Hairston home has become but this one just "hit different."

After months of arguing with Ryan about Bradley's disrespectful ways, she had reached her fill. Earlier that evening, Ryan's 17-year-old son with his college girlfriend Brooke, had crossed the point of no return. During an argument with Blake about bringing girls into their home, an inebriated Bradley spit in her face! After years of raising him as her own and months of her husband defending him, the gesture associated with his action brought Blake to her bursting point. It was better for her and her children to walk away, than to serve life in prison for murder. As she cleansed her face in the mirror of her and Ryan's master bathroom, she saw the reflection of a women whose voice, presence and actions were no longer appreciated. She knew it was time to remove herself from the toxic environment that once nurtured her very soul. She called her cousin Lexi since her parents were away and asked if she would book the suite. As a popular First Lady she didn't want a nosey employee to disclose her whereabouts. She packed clothes for her and the children, woke them out of their sleep and drove to the Oxon Hill, Maryland hotel.

Sitting with Lexi as she relived the events of the previous evening, brought Blake to tears and anger. The demeaning actions of her bonus child turned step-son was followed by a scathing phone call from her mother-in-law Victoria which Blake ended with a dial tone. Victoria had morphed into Blake's prosecutor and Bradley's defense attorney. The filth and moral decay running rampant in Bradley's life was more than she was willing to tolerate. In Ryan's absence, Bradley has become so unbearable that leaving her home in the middle of the night without having to worry about her and the children's safety was refreshing. The children sleep in her room with the door bolted every night Ryan is away. Bradley had become dangerous and unpredictable. She could see the headline now: **"Megachurch First Lady Murders Husband's Son."** She and Ryan were no strangers to controversy but the church is the only institution on the earth that celebrates its own downfall. Church folk love their gossip piping hot and the more scandalous, the better.

Lexi was secretly relieved because Blake would finally have some peace. She listened intently as Blake shared her heart. Lexi was so thankful that God hadn't called her to a life of public service. She looked on for years as Ryan and Blake served selflessly only to be attacked with lies and prejudgment. Articles, news stories and blog posts had been written about their lifestyle. Accusations of mishandling money and the like. Nobody cared that they are landlords, counselors and business owners who generate multiple streams of income. The local news had once run a story adding up the cost of Blake's outfits for one week. Yes, her clothing and accessories had amounted to six-figures but Lexi's sister-in-law Nia was an award-winning fashion designer and celebrity stylist who receives boxes of designer clothes for free. Every season, the women in their family shop in Nia's closets for the newest designer apparel. The family stood amazed that people who benefited from Ryan and Blake's sacrifice weren't wise enough to put 2 and 2 together. Many members who they'd provided shelter, benevolence and transportation to, joined in the lynch mob. Even after the truth would surface, apologies were scarce or nonexistent. The cost alone, was much too high and though Lexi admired her cousin Blake, she had no desire to live in her shoes. She was fine being blasted in reviews by nameless people who she would never meet because her Target™ collection had disappointed their expectations. The cousins cried together as Lexi assured Blake, this too shall pass. After making sure that she was comfortable, Lexi stayed with Blake until she fell asleep and took the extra key card to return later in the day.

34 miles away, Ryan landed at IAD at 5am. He had numerous voice messages from his mother Victoria and his son Bradley. His mother called to bash Blake as she had been doing for almost a year. She told Ryan that she was tired of her grandson being mistreated and was willing to take him in. While listening to Bradley's messages, Ryan could hear the voice of a drunken fool and wondered how his home had become the den of iniquity. The last message was from Paris who told Ryan that Blake and the children were safe at a hotel but that Bradley had spit in his wife's face. Ryan was livid. He called Blake's phone over a dozen times but received no answer. When he pulled into their garage, he saw the empty space that once housed Blake's White Sand Bentley Bentayga V8. Leaving his luggage in the trunk, he headed for Bradley's bedroom. When he entered the house through the kitchen, he could hear the syncopation of a popular rap song. Planning to wear his son out for the ultimate disrespect of his wife, Ryan burst into Bradley's room to find him having sex with a teenage classmate. Startling them both, the young girl ran to cover herself as Bradley sat up in a panic. It was a Wednesday morning during the school year and he asked the young lady where her parents were. She informed Ryan that her mother was cool with her spending the night and Ryan informed her that *he* wasn't cool with it. Liquor bottles and weed paraphernalia were all over the room. He also noticed that Bradley was as bare as a horse with no saddle. Ryan's anger bubbled just below the surface knowing he was in a very vulnerable position. Bradley was too intoxicated to bring the young lady home which left him, a pastor with the task of driving home a teenage girl who had just had sex and indulged in drugs and alcohol under his roof. He paced the floor for

God's wisdom knowing that putting a young girl into a car service alone, wasn't wise. He then called his brother Joshua's house and asked his sister in law Bella, to drive the young girl home. 20 minutes later, Bella pulled up in the driveway and Ryan gave her some money for her trouble. When he went back into the house Bradley had fallen asleep. Ryan commenced to whoop his behind as he should have done months ago.

Crashing and yelling could be heard in the still of the night while Ryan beat his son until he himself was tired. When Ryan stopped to catch his breath, Bradley ran out of the room to vomit from his hangover and assault. Ryan decided to see what had been transpiring under his roof. He tore through Bradley's room and found pornographic magazines and pictures. His phone, desktop, laptop and tablet were flooded with pornographic imagery and content. Cartoons downloaded to his devices were also crude and lascivious. He grew angry and ashamed with himself for disregarding his wife's complaints. She told him she suspected the behaviors of addiction through Bradley's behavior but he disregarded her concerns. Just then his mother called him to talk about Blake. Stopping her in mid-sentence, Ryan told his mother that Bradley spit in Blake's face and that his behavior was beyond disrespectful. Victoria asked Ryan what Blake did to warrant her own treatment because Bradley was a great kid. Ryan quickly corrected his mother and informed her that her days of speaking ill of his wife were over before disconnecting the call. Ryan was so angry. Why does his own family think it's okay to dishonor his wife? Where did it all go wrong?

Ryan called Blake several times throughout the morning without an answer. He called the children's school and found that they weren't present. He knew Paris wouldn't disclose her location but only called as a courtesy, so he waited. Later that evening, Blake returned his call. Ryan apologized profusely and told Blake what he walked into when he arrived at home.

Without acknowledging the situation, Blake informed Ryan that she and her children wouldn't return as long as Bradley resided in their home. She reminded her husband of all the incidents that took place in their home that Ryan made excuses for. He agreed and suggested they get family counseling. Blake made it very clear that there is no counseling for someone who spit in her face. Ryan shuttered at the thought of Bradley demeaning his wife that way. "It's us or him," said Blake before ending the call. Defeated and at wits end, Ryan sat back in his recliner not knowing what to do.

Rhoda walked through the door of Blake's suite up in arms. She couldn't believe her ears when she and Evans touched down at BWI. Nobody spits in her child's face without a day of reckoning. Thankful that they were safe, she hugged Blake so tight before hearing the rumble of little feet running. Her grandchildren were so happy to see her as she came bearing gifts. Ryan Jr. And Rayne were 9 and Royce was 5. They loved Nana Ro. Rhoda let them open their gifts and showed them pictures of her and Grandpa Evans' trip. They were excited to play the Hawaiian version of a boardgame she purchased for them and they pretended to let Royce play. He clapped with joy as the twins kept telling him he won. Once they were settled and content, Rhoda held her full grown baby girl. She had been a witness to Bradley's degradation and Ryan's detachment. It was especially hard to submit to him as her pastor knowing he wasn't governing his house as he should. Rhoda had to keep her heart right before the Lord in order to remain an effective intercessor. She loved Ryan as if he were her very son but his neglect of her daughter had finally come to a head. She watched Blake behind the scenes covering his ministry and name only to go home and not be appreciated. Lady Blake had stopped members from walking out and guarded his reputation at all cost. She remembers when Royce had a knot on his head and told everyone that Bradley threw him down the stairs and Bradley insisted that Royce fell. Rhoda and Blake knew he was lying but Ryan accepted Bradley's explanation as baby Royce could only say "Him throw me down there" while pointing to the staircase. Since then, Blake never left her children unattended around Bradley. The twins also testified that Bradley would take their money and threatened them with harm if they told. If Blake needed to go to the store without the children, she would drive 40 minutes to Rhoda's house just to shop at a store 10 minutes from hers.

Blake told Rhoda that Victoria had changed. All their interactions had turned into back-handed comments to tear Blake down and question her character. Victoria felt as though Blake should get a job and often overly complimented women who "took care of themselves" in Blake's presence. Comments about living off of a man or how shameful it was depending on someone else, always escaped her mouth. Blake may not have been on anyone's payroll but she surely worked. In addition to sound investments that brought income into their home Blake helped raise Ryan's cousin Nia's daughter Nya, Bradley's mother's daughter Davina, Bradley and her own children. She sat on boards, committees, and founded The Light Awards™ which has become the Oscars of public service. She mentors' women, counsels couples and has helped countless marriages to be restored. Blake's work was extensive and far reaching into the most intimate places of people's lives. She has done things for people that only she and God know about yet Victoria sees no value in her roles. Rhoda was heated. In her annoyance, Rhoda commented that Victoria should be "more concerned with Gavin being in Sister Haskin's face than what Blake does with her time." "Joann Haskins?" Blake inquired. "No, Lilly Haskins," Rhoda confirmed. "She's like 35 years old and my father in law is 65," Blake added. "I know how old he is," Rhoda said matter-of-factly. Blake was floored. After the initial shock of picturing Gavin with Lilly Haskins, Blake resolved that she had her own marital problems without taking on the problems of her in-laws'.

Gavin, Evans and Freddie met up at Glory Days in Bowie, for their bi-weekly men's night. Gavin was shocked when Evans informed him that his daughter and their grandchildren were living in a hotel. He was even more shocked to learn that his grandson spit in Blake's face. Gavin knew he was now choosing to "live *his* best life" but made a mental note to have a sit down with Ryan. Freddie added to the story in sharing that Ryan called his daughter Bella who is married to Gavin's other son Joshua to drive a young lady home that Ryan caught in bed with Bradley. Gavin couldn't believe his ears. He was at an age where he just wanted to have peace. Evans and Freddie knew that he was having an affair with Lilly and that he hadn't been happy with Victoria for years. They knew it wouldn't be much longer before Gavin decided to leave. His sons were grown, God-fearing men who had their own families. Gavin put his sons through school, put enough money away to leave them and his grandchildren an inheritance, paid off his wife's home and set her up should anything happen to him. The only missing piece was his own happiness. He had served his family for decades and now it was his turn. The three men shared an unbreakable bond whether right, wrong or indifferent. Each man had their own struggles over the years that the other two saw them through. When Evans broke several men's limbs over monies owed to him, the other two covered him. When Freddie almost lost his house gambling, the other two covered him. When Gavin got a DUI and almost went to jail, the other two covered for him. When Evans was ripped off in a business deal and burnt a man's house to the ground, the other two covered him. When Freddie had a fling with a young college girl, the other two covered him. It was just Gavin's turn again. All three men agreed that Blake needed to feel appreciated in her own home, that Ryan needed this wake-up call and that Bradley needed his tail beat. The three fathers pledged to do their part in order to see Blake healthy and whole, make sure Ryan was shook and that Bradley was straightened out. Evans held a private addendum in his heart to get Bradley "got" and deep-down, Gavin and Freddie knew it.

A few days later, Blake and the kids went over her parent's house so Ryan could see the children. Royce was so excited to see his father but due to his travel schedule, the twins were used to going days without seeing him. They were none the wiser and enjoyed living in the hotel. They could swim every day and liked eating out. Royce clung to his father and wouldn't let go. When Blake walked into the family room, Ryan noticed the indifference in his wife's eyes. When did she stop being excited to see him, he thought to himself? Ryan had a dozen questions without answers. When he approached her for a hug and kiss, it was as bland as ever. As the twins ran around their grandparent's house playing hide and go seek, Royce remained on the couch with his parents. He was a sensitive child and could sense the tension between them.

Ryan asked Blake when her and the children would be back home. Blake grew irritated by his question and asked if his son still resided there. Ryan responded with a question asking Blake where he was supposed to go. Blake looked Ryan square in the eyes and said "he wouldn't be living there if it were *your* face that he spit in," before walking out of the room. Ryan knew she was right. He wasn't even sure if Bradley would be alive. That evening Rhoda cooked a meal fit for royalty to add comfort to their family's storm. She prepared a pot roast with mashed potatoes and gravy, cabbage, carrots and a homemade chocolate cake. It was a cold Saturday in November and Ryan hadn't prepared a message for the following day. He's spent the past few days wondering where it all went wrong.

Seeing his dismay, Evans told Ryan to join him in the basement. Ryan followed him down to his man cave as tears flooded his eyes. Evans turned on some classic jazz and sat across from Ryan in his favorite recliner. Offering him no comfort, Evans asked Ryan what he planned to do to ensure the safety of his daughter and grandchildren. Ryan shrugged his shoulders and shook his head. Evans told Ryan that not knowing what to do was unacceptable. He then asked Ryan where Brooke was, seeing as though she *is* his mother. For the first time in years Ryan realized that Brooke hadn't played a major role in Bradley's life and therefore should be happy to assist. Ryan told Evans that he wondered where Bradley got the unmitigated gall to disrespect his wife. "From you" Evans replied with an "in your face" attitude. "You showed that boy that my daughter's voice and opinion doesn't matter every time you disregard her feelings and concerns." Evans added. "The fact that you were fool enough to believe that his ignorant behind didn't throw my grandson down those stairs, proves that. Did you know that my daughter and grandchildren lock themselves in your bedroom every night you're away because we have no idea what his drug addicted, drunken, sexually perverted behind is capable of?" Evans unleashed. "I keep my ear to the streets and know for a fact that your boy is beyond marijuana and beer," said Evans. "Blake has to drive all the way over here just to be able to go to the store without the children. I didn't give you my daughter's hand in marriage for her to live in *The War of the Roses*." Evans chided. "You get that fool out of my daughter's house or she's living with me," Evans finished. Ryan had no response. He just cried. He cried for the fear his wife and children were living with, he cried for the degradation of his son's young life and he cried because Mr. Blake Evans was a thug from way back and he knew not to play games with him. That evening Rhoda packed up a take home container for Ryan and told him she'd see him at church. Evans and Blake made no plans to attend Sunday service. Royce cried when his father left and the twins just joyfully said goodbye. Ryan told Blake that he would see them the following day. Once Ryan left, Evans told Blake that her and the children were to move out of the MGM and stay with him and Rhoda. They drove to the National Harbor to pack Blake and the children's belongings and Lexi met them there to check-out and reconcile the bill. Once back at the house, Blake settled into the second master bedroom and the children settled into their room that Rhoda established was theirs since they were born. Royce would sleep wherever he wanted and chose to be with his mom.

The following morning Blake felt so free. She couldn't remember the last time she had a day off from church. She also couldn't remember what she used to do on Sundays prior to her conversion so long ago. Rhoda and the children were already at GLC. As the Church Treasurer and Department Director of the Intercessors, Sundays were work days for Rhoda. The children would attend children's church or sit in the sanctuary to hear their father's message. Either way, Blake wasn't stepping foot into God's Love Church until its senior leader ran his home in the same excellence. After a long bath using her favorite products from *Jo Malone London*, Blake slathered her skin in the brand's Nectarine Blossom and Honey body creme. As she sat at the vanity, she followed her facial skin regimen with the *Kiehl's Ultra* line. After her skin was prepped, she used her curling wand to add some texture to her jet-black bob. As she styled her hair, she decided she would make an appointment with her hair stylist, Anastasia for some color and highlights. After her hair was finished, she took out a flat top kabuki brush and put on her favorite *Nars Radiant Long-*

wear Foundation in the color Syracuse. She groomed her eyebrows before choosing eyeshadow colors from her *Urban Decay Naked Heat Palette.* She followed up her makeup look with a Bronzer by *Fenty Beauty* and her current favorite lip combo of M.A.C.'s *My Tweedy* lipstick with a swipe of *C*-Thru *lipglass.* Once her face was flawless, she spritzed her pulse points with *Baccarat Rouge 540 Extrait.* She chose to wear a pair of black leather leggings, a black camisole and a belted black cashmere sweater coat. She added a short stack to her left wrist with her *Rolex Oystersteel Lady-Datejust*, a white gold and diamond *Cartier Juste un Clou* and a white gold *Cartier Love Bracelet.* On her right wrist she always wore her *Tiffany and Co* charm bracelet from the children. She grabbed her bag of the day, the large *Lady Dior Cannage* in matte black and slipped into her black Chanel lace-up combat boots. When she opened her parent's front door, she was greeted by sunshine. She took in a deep breath to enjoy the crisp fall air that always energized her soul. While standing in her moment of freedom a light breeze danced across her face as she heard the chime of a neighbor's wind ornaments in the distance. She was all dressed up with nowhere to go. Just then her phone vibrated with a call from Lexi. Before she could speak Lexi asked "We going to brunch or nah." "We're going" Blake exclaimed. "I'm 2 minutes out" Lexi sang back. Blake smiled as she hung up the phone. Just seconds later she saw Lexi's shiny new custom *Diamondberry* GLS 550 Mercedes pull into her parent's driveway. Lexi's husband Paris and father-in-law Parrish own 7 luxury car dealerships throughout Virginia. Their most lucrative location *Lovehall Mercedes* in Northern Virginia is the location her husband Paris works from. When Lexi's bedding collection sold out across the country she decided to trademark and patent a color she developed called Diamondberry. The deep magenta shade with rose gold reflects was an instant hit. Since then, everything from pots and pans to rugs were offered in the beautiful hue. The color was also incorporated into a makeup collaboration between Lexi and celebrity makeup artist Beat by Shay. Blake hopped into the truck and the sister cousins were off to celebrate her new found freedom. Their first stop was brunch at the Four Seasons. The two ladies noshed on gourmet cuisine and talked about Blake's new plans to put herself first. Ryan was about to find out how much his devoted wife held up the life he took for granted. Though her presence was no longer felt, her absence was sure to rock his entire world. Lexi made mental notes to make sure she had a life too, her children Pierre and Paris Jr. needed her to be whole in order to serve them. Blake looked around at all the happy faces in the room. She was living life all wrong, Sunday was the new Friday! After brunch the ladies found themselves at Tyson's Corner where they each spent 4 figures in 2 hours without blinking. They justified their purchases by throwing in a few Christmas gifts. After a full day of fun, Lexi brought Blake back to her Auntie Rhoda and Uncle Evans home with plans to do it again each and every Sunday.

Miles away Ryan struggled through his second sermon of the day. His laptop wasn't charged and he couldn't find his cord. As he glanced at the empty seat usually occupied by his wife, he wondered how long she would keep her stance. They were called to serve the people and she had abandoned her post. As people stood up and shouted during his points, his leaders could tell he was off his game and spent the service praying for him. When four people accepted Christ, Ryan didn't have his wife there to welcome them to the family of God. When two families joined the church, he dryly announced that he and his family honored the pleasure of serving them. Ryan was cranky and hungry. Blake always made sure his breakfast was ready and his bag was packed. His afternoon meal wasn't waiting for him and his shoes were too tight. He just wanted to go home and crawl into bed but he had three counseling sessions back to back. The first session was Mother Lee who was raising her drug addicted daughter's teenagers at 82 years old, the second was his spiritual son Elder Lawson Taylor and his last session was brother and sister Gilbert who wanted a divorce.

Ryan shifted in his chair half listening to Mother Lee. He heard something about the teen's new friends, some hours of detention and a broken window. His mind was on his own family and especially his wife. He knew he had to do something to make things right because he needed things to go back to the way they use to be. Snorting and crying into her hanky, Mother Lee looked to him for a solution. Ryan asked her what she wanted him to do. Mother Lee asked him if the girls could go back to the program First Lady signed them up for. Ryan had no idea what she was speaking of. "They did so well during their time there," Mother Lee expressed. Ryan told her he would find out what the dates were for the program and get back to her. Mother Lee asked if First Lady would still be willing to pay the cost because she didn't have the $3000.00 the program required. Ryan told Mother Lee it would be taken care of. Lastly, she asked for her grocery money, As Ryan was about to inquire about what grocery money she spoke of, Rhoda knocked on the glass door of his counseling room. When he motioned his mother in law to enter, she excused herself and gave Mother Lee an envelope from Blake. Mother Lee was so grateful. Blake had been supplementing her Social Security income, because it wasn't enough to support herself and 2 teenage girls. Ryan had no idea that his wife had been doing so and wished Mother Lee well. When she left Ryan expressed to Rhoda that Blake never mentioned her monthly contribution to help Mother Lee. "Son, you'll soon find out that my daughter holds this entire church together," Rhoda said in her feisty fashion before closing the door behind her. Ryan had no time to ponder what had just happened before his brother Joshua opened the door to let Elder Lawson into the room for his next session. Ryan sat again half listening as Lawson laid out his concerns. Something about Ava's spending habits and their investments. Reminding Ryan of the time he once paid for his groceries when he was at rock bottom and Ava driving them to the poor house. Ryan thought about Blake and how frustrated he was that she was making a power play. He was still her husband and it was time for the foolery to end. He would call Brooke and tell her to come get her child so Blake and the children would come home. When Lawson stopped talking, Ryan asked him what he wanted him to do. He told him he'd like for First Lady to speak to Ava because she was a better wife when she was in Blake's mentoring program. Ryan told Lawson he would have Blake reach out to her and Lawson was grateful. Ryan asked Lawson if he'd been studying since the last time they spoke, about his call to preach. Lawson said he has and Ryan told him he was to preach both services next Sunday and Lawson was honored. Ryan sat in silence for the few minutes he had before Joshua brought Draya and Keoin Gilbert into the counseling room. The couple greeted him before handing him 2 envelopes. When Ryan asked what they were, Sister Gilbert told him it was their son Kaleb's report card in one and a check for First Lady in the other. Ryan saw with his own eyes that Kaleb's grades went from C's and D's to straight A's. Wow! Ryan exclaimed. Yes, the Gilberts said in unison. "When our business failed and we lost everything, having to move back in with my in-laws," Keoin expressed, "First Lady paid for his tuition while we got back on our feet. He struggled during the transition but the tutor she got him, has him back on track. We had to return to our government jobs but we wanted to pay her back for all her assistance." Ryan peaked inside the envelope to see an $8k check for his wife. "If you made it through the storm, why do you want a divorce?" Ryan asked. "Because her mother is the third person in our marriage and I'm tired of it," Keoin said switching his demeanor from calm to indignant. "What married woman takes marital advice from a woman whose never been married nor can even keep a man?" Keoin exclaimed. "Ryan looked at Draya who said, "she's only picking because we live there Pastor." Ryan sat up in his chair and said "move out" with a confused look on his face. "If you have no peace where you reside, just leave." As Ryan said the words conviction had overtaken him. It was the exact choice that his wife made and he grew ashamed. In a teachable moment, Ryan expressed to the Gilberts that his drug addicted son has wreaked havoc in their home causing First Lady to move out. His transparency nourished them in a way that his messages never could. They agreed to just get an apartment for their peace than to sacrifice their covenant, trying to save up for a house. Ryan assured them if they had it and lost it, they could get it back again. "Now you have the benefit of experience and understanding" Ryan counseled." Unfortunately, life gives us the test before the lesson but you two have what it takes to recover" Ryan added. The Gilberts agreed and saw their Pastor in a whole new light. Ryan prayed for them before ending their session and thanked them for helping him just as much.

Ryan walked to his office and took two Aleve before he dialed Brooke. When she answered, he told her what happened. She expressed to him that if Blake wasn't safe around Bradley and she raised him, then she didn't want Bradley in her house either. He told her it was the least she could do as his mother. Feeling the shade Ryan was throwing her way, Brooke asked him how Bradley could be raised in a 2 parent, upper middle-class home with a Pastor for a father and end up a thug when he was a manurable and happy child while raised by a single mom. Ryan grew annoyed by her retaliation and told her it was because she abandoned him to be a reality star. She called him a hypocrite; he called her a thot. She told him he wasn't fit to run a church if he couldn't run his house and he hung up on her. Ryan had been hit where it hurts and

Brook was humiliated. She wished she had never met him since he couldn't find it in his heart to express the love of Christ toward her. He was offended that she called him out on something he already knew was true. Miles apart, the onetime college lovers had managed to wound each other instead of coming to a solution for the child they shared. They each ached silently knowing they weren't their best for him and didn't know where to begin to pick up the pieces of his shattered, young life. Ryan called his mother and told her that he would take her up on her offer to house Bradley but that he also needed to go to rehab. Victoria told Ryan that Bradley wasn't an addict and that he had fallen for the lies of his wife. Ryan warned her to tread lightly and she agreed to pick him and his belongings up that evening.

Later that evening after a hot meal from Whole Foods and a long shower, Ryan called Blake. Hearing her voice, made him warm and fuzzy. Instead of talking about their problems he asked her if he was still going to receive conjugal visits. She told him she wasn't a fool and said yes. He asked if she was willing to come over and she asked if his house had been exterminated. When he told her it had been, she agreed. She offered to be there in an hour. Ryan smiled and planned on putting it down so she would come home. When Blake arrived, Ryan opened the garage entrance door greased up with baby oil wearing his gray sweatpants. Though she was still hurt she had to admit that her husband was beautiful. The past few years had blessed him with some gray hairs on his head and beard that complimented his smooth chocolate skin. That evening, they made love like it was their honeymoon. The love between them was explosive and Ryan realized how much he needed her. Her body was his refuge and his arms were hers. The following morning Blake asked if they could get a new house because so many bad memories were locked within its walls. Ryan told her no. He told her there was no need to buy a new house when new memories could outweigh the bad ones. An argument ensued. Blake told Ryan that he hadn't appreciated her in so long that it was the least he could do. Ryan told Blake that she abandoned her post as First Lady and left him high and dry. Blake accused him of putting the church before his family, expressing that he's gone so much that the twins don't even miss him. The couple went tit for tat for over 2 hours until they sat on either side of their marriage bed exhausted. The final blow to Blake's heart was when Ryan said, "Just tell me what store the bag or shoes or jewelry is in; so, I can buy it and you can come home." Blake stood up and began to put on her clothes. "Are you serious right now?" Blake exclaimed "You and your miserable mother actually think I can be bought? You're about to find out that I'm not the one." Blake promised. Ryan felt the shift in the room and tried to apologize. When their eyes met, he saw the pain of a weary woman. Tears were streaming down his face as he tried to hold her and repent. He knew he went too far. He held her and kissed her to no avail. When she broke free, she grabbed a suitcase from her side of the closet and packed up more clothes and shoes. As she walked down the stairs, he tried to stop her from leaving. She could barely see through her tears but managed to find the kitchen door that leads to the garage. He apologized profusely and said he would make it right while holding the door closed above her head. Remembering the envelopes from the Gilberts, he placed them in her hand from his briefcase sitting on the floor. As she received them, he grabbed her suitcase and opened the door. Still naked, he sat her luggage in the backseat as she climbed into the driver's seat. As she turned the ignition and the garage door began to open, he ran inside before his body was exposed to the frigid November air. "I love you" were the last words he spoke as Blake drove away. It was a Monday morning just over a week before Thanksgiving and the Hairston family was officially fractured.

Victoria was so glad to have Bradley in the house. Gavin was coming home less and less and she could use the company. She was about to show her son and his high-saddity wife, that all he needed was love. These new parents had no idea how to raise children and especially when the so-called mother is more concerned about being cute than raising sound children. Victoria wasn't crazy about Bella either but at least she had a job. Blake had been living off her son for over a decade and she needed to get off the couch and do something, Victoria thought. What dignified woman sits around while a man takes care of her. She wanted to stay home with Ryan and Joshua as babies, but Gavin told her, he needed her to work and contribute to their household. Blake was exactly the kind of woman that Victoria couldn't respect. A pampered princess. One thing is for sure, Blake wasn't getting a dime of her hard earned money. When she wrote her will, she left Blake completely out of it. While Victoria was rehearsing her disdain for Blake, Bradley had cut school with the young lady next door. He forgot how pretty Tia Edwards was. Her family lived next door from Victoria and Gavin for years, but Bradley didn't notice her until he saw her outside yesterday evening. Her father was in the military and her mother had another family, so she lived with her grandmother Barbara. They'd been having sex and getting high all morning. He knew she was down when he saw the look in her eyes. They were on the phone all night. He couldn't leave because Victoria hadn't given him the alarm code, so he had to wait until it was time to leave for school. Tia was mixed and had long hair that smelled like strawberries. Bradley loved girls who didn't try to make him wait. This was going to be a great new situation for him. The two lovers did pills, smoked opioids and snorted cocaine. Thanksgiving came and went without any fanfare. Rhoda cooked her usual spread, but the family didn't gather in the grand manner of holidays past. Ryan, Joshua, Bella and the children joined them. Freddie and Gavin didn't show, and Rhoda didn't extend an invitation to Victoria. The Virginia clan stayed home and Mumzie and Grandpa Rhodes were probably up to no good. The family played board games, watched football, and ended with some movies suitable for the children. Ryan and Blake made up for the time being, but Ryan knew deep work had to be done.

2

THE SCORE

*B*radley struggled to breath as a group of boys beat him senseless. Sweating profusely and begging for his life, the kicking and punching finally stopped. He took the train into DC like he did every week to cop some drugs but was dragged into an alley. They must have him confused with someone else because he didn't know who they were. Bleeding from his mouth and clenching his side, Bradley struggled to stand. When he stood, one of the boys' spit in his face and knocked him back to the ground. Instantly Bradley knew he was being paid back for what he did to Blake. Fear gripped him knowing only one person was capable of ordering such a beat down. As he laid in the alley crying and scared, one of the perpetrators stood over him and urinated. When the group finally walked away, Bradley reached in his pocket to call 911. Sitting across the street from the alley in an F-150 pickup borrowed from a friend, Evans watched the entire ordeal before driving away in satisfaction.

.   .   .

Victoria rushed to Washington Medical Center to be by Bradley's side. She called Ryan on the way and he was right behind her. Bradley had suffered 3 fractured ribs, a bruised kidney and loss 4 teeth. When his grandmother and father arrived, Bradley told them he took the train to DC to get his favorite wings and some boys approached him for money. He added that when he told them no, they beat him up and left him for dead. Victoria began to cry but Ryan grew suspicious. Victoria promised him that she'd take good care of him but Ryan asked, "what wing place?" Bradley knew his father had finally accepted the truth and was upset by his indifference. Ignoring his father's question, Bradley poured it on thick for the doting of his grandmother. She believed every word he said no matter how unreasonable. Ryan walked out of the room and went to the nurse's station. He asked if a full drug panel could be performed on Bradley and they agreed. Moments later, a nurse came into the room to draw some vials of blood. Bradley knew immediately what Ryan had done and grew angry. To gain more points with Victoria, a manipulative Bradley began to cry. He told his grandmother that Ryan didn't like him and how Blake turned his father against him. Victoria turned to Ryan and told him to look at what that "trick" has done to his child. Ryan was jolted by Victoria's statement and looked at her with disgust in his eyes. Bradley smirked as Ryan's blood boiled. Victoria was provoking Ryan to wrath, and he envisioned himself knocking her to the floor. She'd better thank God that he had too much to lose, he thought. Victoria told Ryan to leave if he didn't have sympathy for his own son. Ryan, saying nothing walked out of the room. He asked the head nurse to call him with the results before driving back to Maryland. The following morning, Ryan arranged for a meeting with Brooke. He spoke to Blake about what happened and had her permission to meet Brooke for breakfast. While Ryan sat in the small café waiting for Brooke, she entered wearing a tracksuit with her hair in a top knot. Brooke looks like LisaRaye and Ryan remembered the first time he saw her on campus. Brooke approached the table and Ryan stood up to greet her. The two embraced and Brooke could smell the *Clive Christian* cologne Ryan was wearing. Brooke was a few inches taller than Blake so in reaching for her waist during the hug, Ryan actually grabbed her butt. He apologized and Brooke said it wasn't a problem. Ryan pulled out her chair and tried not to notice how well Brooke was built. When the waiter arrived, they both ordered the steak and eggs. Ryan started the conversation by apologizing to Brooke. He admitted that he was disrespectful and trying to hurt her feelings. She accepted and apologized for the part she played. He told her about Bradley's behavior and drug abuse. He took full responsibility for Bradley's downward spiral and asked Brooke if she'd partner with him to help their son. Brooke expressed to Ryan that though she felt helpless and had younger children to care for, she'd do what she can. Brooke confided in Ryan about Victoria leaving her messages to steal him from Blake. Ryan was floored. Perceiving her vulnerability Ryan told Brooke "You fine but I'm married." Everyone knew that Victoria has always been partial to Brooke, including Blake but Ryan never regretted choosing his wife. Brooke told Ryan how much she appreciated Blake and how she'd never disrespect her. Ryan was convicted by Brooke's loyalty to Blake since he hasn't had her back as he should. Ryan knew he had a remarkable woman and made a mental note to show her how much she was appreciated. During breakfast, the doctor called to tell Ryan that opioids', marijuana and cocaine were found in Bradley's system. He also told Ryan that Victoria had taken him home against his recommendations. Ryan thanked the doctor before ending the call. Ryan told Brooke about the doctor's findings and what his mother had done. Brooke was saddened by the news and continued their meal in silence. After they ate Ryan walked Brooke to her car. Tears began to stream down her face and Ryan felt her pain. No matter how distant he saw a mother's love in her eyes. Ryan held her in the parking lot for what seemed like half an hour. When she gathered herself together, Ryan kissed her on the forehead and shut her door. Brooke started her car and backed away before driving out of the lot and turning around the corner. Ryan was exhausted!

Across town when Blake ended her call with Ryan, Rhoda was making everyone's plate for breakfast. She asked Blake if everything was okay. Without thinking about the children's presence Blake told Evans and Rhoda that Bradley had been jumped in an alley and hospitalized. She added that Ryan was meeting Brooke for breakfast to discuss what should be done about him. "That's too bad," Rhoda said sincerely while looking across the table at her husband. Evans was disappointed that there was no mention of spit or piss but he had the satisfaction of knowing that Bradley knew.

A few weeks later, Ryan walked around Tyson's corner shopping for the children's Christmas gifts. He decided to buy Blake a special gift because of his snide remarks. He knew it was wrong to pretend that a material possession could solve their marital issues but also found it interesting, when Blake mentioned his mother believing she could be bought. Ryan didn't realize his mother could be so cruel. Blake told Ryan several times that he knew Victoria as his mother, not as a woman. He was sinking deeper into a funk and didn't know the way out. He thought about the twins and how much of their lives he missed out on when his traveling engagements increased. Earlier that morning while Ryan was in prayer, he knew his prayers had bounced off the ceiling and fallen to the ground; return to sender. He needed the advice of a neutral party. Someone who has been in Blake's shoes. Immediately he thought of Lady Celestine Kemp and decided he would phone her later that evening. While eating in the food court he saw his Aunt Pat and Uncle Parrish but let them walk by without getting their attention. When he saw his cousin Courtney and her husband Texan, he decided to leave the galleria before someone spotted him. When he got back to his car, he decided to phone Apostle Sands to see if he could get a last-minute counseling session and was so thankful that the man of God agreed.Back in Maryland, Blake was submitting all of her roles to a friend of Evans and Rhoda who specialized in writing resumes. With a degree from Towson University and a diverse collection of experience, she was sure to find a new opportunity. Blake has been working for her husband for more than a decade without a salary and it was time to do something for herself. She knew it would change the dynamics of her family to be a working mother, but nobody was about to write her off as worthless! She was more willing than ever to show Ryan how much his life would change without her at GLC from day to day. How dare he reduce her role in his life to the items in her closet. She wasn't that far removed from the days she and Rhoda faced after her biological father Kenneth left. There were many days when money was scarce and they had to make do. Blake and Rhoda were finally in a good place when Evans entered their lives. He was a godsend. The level of protection and love that he has for them is second to none. To this day, most people have no idea that Evans isn't Blake's biological father. Evans would bring harm to the person who would dare say Blake wasn't his daughter and she felt the same way. Having the same first name also lends to their special bond. She knew she could stay at her parents' home forever and a day but Ryan had gone too far.

When Ryan arrived at the Sands' home in Woodbridge, Virginia he knew he was in a safe place. Over the years Apostle

Sands and Lady Eleanor had become like grandparents since his grandmother and Blake's grandfather were off the chain. When he stepped out of the car, he was greeted at the door by their smiling faces. Once inside, tears began to stream from his eyes. Eleanor handed Ryan a box of tissue and asked the housekeeper to bring him a beverage. He and Apostle Sands made small talk before Ryan shared his heart. He told his mentor how Blake and the children moved to her parent's house, how Bradley spit in her face and that his life was spiraling out of control. Ryan expressed that he lost his family in pursuit of ministry and had made so many horrible mistakes. Apostle Sands was no stranger to the woes of men in ministry and listened before asking Ryan "who is she?" Confused by his question, Ryan asked, "Who is who?" Apostle Sands responded in a confrontational voice "The woman you're sleeping with." "I'm not, nor have I ever, cheated on Blake, Granddad," Ryan responded. Annoyance came over Apostle Sands' face. "You mean to tell me you allowed your wife to leave instead of putting that fool out of your home? I know Blake entirely too well to know she wouldn't just leave without giving you many opportunities to get it right." Apostle Sands said sternly. Ryan shook his head in agreement. He told him how Blake and the children would lock themselves in the bedroom while he was away, that Bradley was a drug addict and how he threw Royce down the stairs. Ryan was ashamed that he ignored Blake's pleas for help and the disappointment in Apostle Sands' face. "You are the first Pastor in my 60 plus years of ministry whose wife didn't walk out because of another woman, so I honor your integrity," Apostle Sands said. Ryan thanked him and took out a pen and paper as he was instructed to do. For the following 3 hours he gleaned the wisdom of his spiritual grandfather to put his home back together.

. . .

It was Sunday funday, when Blake and Lexi decided to drive to King of Prussia Mall for some retail therapy. While walking through the food court they ran into Lady Celestine. Lady C embraced Blake and was so surprised to see her. She asked Blake how things were going and immediately tears began to stream down her face. Lady Celestine was taken back and told Blake that they needed to talk. Blake agreed as she wiped her eyes and promised to call her in the morning. Lexi felt Blake's pain and they decided to end their day and drive back to Maryland. During the ride home, Blake rehearsed her conversation with Lady C in her head. She knew if anyone understood the woes of being a leading lady, it was Lady Celestine Kemp. By the time the sister cousins reached Rhoda and Evans' subdivision they were upbeat and joyful. Lexi put on Blake's favorite songs by Drake and they sang along and danced in their seats. When Lexi pulled into the driveway, Blake saw Ryan's car parked outside. Butterflies filled her stomach at the thought of seeing him. She was so in love with Ryan but she knew she had to play hardball in order for her needs to be met. When they entered the house, Royce ran up to his mom with a smile on his face. He was such a loving and affectionate child who brought joy to her life. After greeting everyone, Lexi went to the bathroom before heading back to Alexandria. When Blake entered her bedroom to put her bags down Ryan was asleep in her bed. She noticed that he lost weight and that his socks were mismatched. It was 3 days before Christmas and they needed a miracle. Rhoda called Royce to come eat dinner and he ran excitedly down the hall. Blake went into the ensuite to use the restroom. When she returned to the bedroom, Ryan was waiting for her in his birthday suit and was extremely happy to see her. Blake blushed and crawled into bed to enjoy her real-life candy bar. After a great time of love making, Ryan and Blake showered together and got dressed to get a plate of food and join the family for Sunday movie night. The children chose the first movie while eating dessert in their pajamas. When the children went to bed, Evans, Rhoda, Blake and Ryan ate their dessert and watched *Truth Be Told*. Ryan had missed so many movies due to his travel schedule so when the women went to bed, he and Evans also watched *MA*. That night Royce slept in the bedroom with the twins and Ryan slept beside his wife. He was given a strict code of conduct by Apostle Sands who told him it would get worse before it gets better but to stay the course. The following morning, Ryan and Blake went Christmas shopping before deciding to have lunch. Blake couldn't remember the last time she sat across the table from her husband in a restaurant. They'd been at odds over Bradley for so long that they hadn't spent any time alone. After a peaceful morning and afternoon, Ryan brought Blake back to the house and told her he'd return later that evening. While wrapping gifts and playing with the children, Blake's phone rang. It was Lady Celestine. Blake walked back to her bedroom to receive the call. After a bit of small talk, Lady C asked Blake what was wrong. She told her that she and the children were living with her parents and that her marriage was on the rocks. "Who's the dirty heifer?" Lady C asked. "He's not cheating," Blake responded and told Lady C how Bradley spit in her face. Lady Celestine looked at the phone in shock and relief. "What kind of vile human being spits on their mama?" Lady C exclaimed. "I know what it's like to raise your husband's child as your own and have him turn around and disrespect you." Lady C shared with Blake some strategies for holding Ryan accountable. Before she hung up, she apologized for assuming a woman had come between them. In her 40 years of being a First Lady she has counseled countless women through the pain of infidelity. Blake understood and accepted Lady C's apology. Giggles and excitement filled the Evans' home as the children opened their gifts. It was Christmas morning and their favorite day of the year. Rayne had hit the sparkle jackpot as everything she wanted was bedazzled. Ryan Jr. was ecstatic to have die cast models of his favorite luxury cars. Royce clapped as he opened gift after gift bearing his favorite characters from *The Secret Life of Pets*. He had the toothbrush, bathrobe, towel, cup, plate, bowl, and bedding. All the children sighed at the sight of new socks and under garments. The family decided to keep it low key since Christmas was in the middle of the week and planned to be together during the weekend. Evans gifted Rhoda with a trip to Tokyo in April and she bought him monogrammed golf clubs. Blake gifted Ryan with a *Moncler* coat and boots and some Chanel Cologne. Thinking along the same lines, Ryan bought Blake a Silver Fox fur coat and some of her favorite body products. That evening during dinner he called his parents to wish them well. When his mother answered they spoke briefly. She didn't have much to say if she wasn't allowed to talk about Blake. He asked about his father and Bradley. Victoria lied and told him that Gavin was taking a nap and Bradley was in his room listening to music. Ryan ended the call and told her he'd stop by the following day.

Across town Gavin was drinking whiskey while Lilly was performing a Christmas strip tease. He installed a pole in their bedroom and Lilly put on shows nightly. Before she was converted by a GLC outreach, Lilly was an accomplished nude dancer at a DC club. Gavin was having the time of his life! Exotic dancers had come a long way since his military days and his sweet Lilly made him feel 20 again. Evans often told Gavin that Lilly will send him to an early grave because she was way too young but Gavin brushed it off as hate. What did Evans know anyway? Rhoda could never do the tricks Lilly could. He snickered to himself as Lilly crawled up to him before kneeling on a pillow...

At the same time, Bradley laid on the mattress of a local Meth house having unprotected sex with two grown women and getting high. He hadn't been home in days. Though he had missing teeth, he felt no pain from his injuries sustained in the alley. He robbed his grandmother of $1500 dollars and immediately called his friends. They understood him and loved him just the way he was. They were the ones who helped him escape the glaring eye of being a PK. He was tired of pretending to be perfect. He met his homeboys Cameron and Jerry at a community outreach GLC was hosting with area churches. Jerry's parents are pastors and he and Bradley hit it off immediately. Cameron's father is a politician and his mother, a popular news anchor. Cameron's family are members of Jerry's parent's church. All of them agree that church isn't for them and that being a so-called Christian is too hard. Bradley has seen Ryan and Blake get dragged through the mud by the same people who sat at their dinner table, given money to and all the horrible rumors that they endure. He believes they are fools for still caring for people while getting stabbed in the back. The boys agreed to live their life for themselves and were introduced into a life of drugs by some cheerleaders who invited them to a house party. Prior to meeting them, the boys hadn't ever been with a white girl so they all went out of curiosity. Before they knew it, they were cutting school and hooking up with them. One of the girls, Jenna, who dated Cameron lives in a mansion with a wait staff. Her parents are never home and leave her and her older siblings to fend for themselves. Bradley dated Heather and Jerry dated Abby until one afternoon the lines got blurred and the girls told them it was okay to hook up in any combination. Since then, the once innocent boys have taken the bait and continue to struggle on the hook. Cameron's parents have put him in treatment only for him to run away from the facility and rejoin the other two. Jerry's parents as Ryan have been too busy serving their ministry to notice his downward spiral.

Blake sat in Rhoda's office filling out the longest online job application of her life. Evans has a military buddy who is about to retire from the government and offered to hire Blake before he leaves. She would only have to fill out the application and come in for the interview for appearance sake. He told Blake if she got everything in by December 31st, he could order her background check and get her clearance to begin working on February 1st. She would be the supervisor over a team of researchers. Her degree in combination with her previous job at the Library of Congress made her a great fit for the position. Blake was excited to be her own woman.Not many miles away, Ryan pulled up to Victoria's house. He noticed that she didn't put up her holiday décor. He knocked on the door instead of using his key. Victoria answered the door with a shocked look on her face. When he asked what was wrong, she told him she was surprised to see him. Ryan reminded his mother that he told her he was coming. Noticing that there was no tree up or any gifts in sight, he asked where his father was. She told Ryan that he went out with Freddie and Evans. When he asked where the gifts were, she told Ryan they had some unexpected expenses with the house. Ryan told his mother that they should've told him and he would've given them some money. Victoria brushed it off and offered him some coffee. He accepted and sat at the kitchen island. When he noticed there was no food in the fridge, he offered to take her to the market. Ryan was puzzled. In all his years on the earth he'd never seen a bare refrigerator in his parent's house. Tight meant that they had to go without extras not basics. His mother agreed to let him buy groceries and went to change her clothes. While Ryan sat at the island drinking his coffee, he heard the thump of the same song Bradley was playing the night he came home. Ryan stood up and looked out the front window. Bradley was getting out of a Bentley coup driven by a young Caucasian girl. Soon after Tia Edwards from next door approached him and an argument ensued. The girl he came with, got out of the car to approach her. They began arguing about whose man he was before fighting outside on Victoria's lawn. Bradley took out his phone and recorded it for his social media account. Ryan noticed how dirty and filthy Bradley was. He also questioned the intelligence of both girls before realizing all three of them were high out of their minds. Ryan couldn't believe his eyes. Bradley was emaciated and scruffy. Tia and the driver were rolling around on the grass. When Victoria asked what was going on, Ryan told her his drug addicted son and his 2 drug addicted girlfriends were making a scene in front of her house. Victoria immediately snapped and told Ryan nothing was wrong with Bradley and that Ryan had been listening to his B#$%^ of a wife. Ryan turned around and told Victoria that she may be his mother but to never call his wife out of her name again. Victoria provoked him some more and told Ryan that she was a gold-digging tramp who needed to get a job. "You and your brother always seen me go to work, yet you let that bimbo walk around here dressed to the nines like she's better than everybody," Victoria yelled. "Don't you dare call my wife a bimbo Ma, I'm not gonna tell you again," Ryan argued. "Forget you and that lazy woman if you're gonna let her come between us," Victoria yelled. Ryan put on his coat and walked out the front door. Before getting in the car he forced Bradley, who was now laying on the grass with both girls, into his back seat.Leaving both girls and Victoria watching in disbelief, he drove away. Ryan drove around until he saw an empty parking lot and pulled over. Ryan went through his phone looking for a community partner's phone number who served those struggling with addiction. Apologizing for calling right after the holiday, Dr. Dante France assured Ryan that the day and time doesn't matter and told Ryan where to meet him. Dr. France was going to call ahead to his facility to prepare for Bradley's arrival. Ryan plugged the address into the navigation and just like that Bradley's intervention had begun. 40 minutes later Ryan drove up to the inpatient juvenile facility and Dante was waiting for him in the lobby. Bradley who must've gotten high again on the grass was out of his mind. He laughed and howled like a wolf when they strapped him to the gurney. Ryan had tears streaming down his face as Dr. France escorted him to his office. Dante comforted Ryan by reminding him how valuable GLC was in the building of the facility. Ryan filled out the intake forms and committed Bradley to the longest treatment available, 90 days. That evening, in tears and defeat, Ryan went back to his in-law's house and cried in his wife's arms. Blake wept alongside him because their son's life hung in the balance. They had sacrificed so much in service to others that they lost their own child in the process. Ryan took full responsibility as Blake did everything she was supposed to do. He didn't tell her about Victoria's comments though she wouldn't be surprised. In the morning, Ryan planned on contacting Bradley's principal personally to find out where he left off. The following morning, Ryan sat in his office at the church and phoned Dr. Maiya Mullen, the head mistress of Potomac Academy. Dr. Mullen greeted Ryan cheerfully but told him that Victoria brought the papers he signed and had notarized when Bradley was expelled for drinking on school grounds. Ryan was livid! His mother's actions not only meant that she is aware of his issue but that she's complicit in his addiction. He thanked the good doctor for her time and wished her a happy New Year. Blake was floored when he told her that Bradley was expelled and Victoria covered it up. Where has he been enrolled? Ryan thought. Ryan immediately called his father with no answer. He called Joshua who had no idea as well. He reluctantly called his mother who defiantly said the school they picked out had him under too much pressure and that he goes to public school. Ryan was even more upset because she was still justifying Bradley's behavior. "Where's my father?" Ryan asked. "At the store," Victoria answered. Ryan told her he'd talk to her later and Victoria asked where Bradley was, when Ryan told her in "rehab" she blew a fuse! "You gon let your so called wife convince you to put my grandson away," Victoria yelled before Ryan hung up the phone. Immediately after he hung up, Victoria called Brooke. When she answered, Victoria told Brooke that Ryan put Bradley in rehab and that nothing is wrong with him. Brooke told Victoria that Bradley spit in Blake's face so something had to be wrong with him. Victoria told Brooke that Blake was a filthy dog who had it out for her grandson and not to trust what she says. Brooke told Victoria that she respects her like a mother but that nobody could talk to her about Blake in that manner and if she's looking for a cosigner it isn't her. Brooke wished her a Happy New Year and ended the call. Victoria was fuming! She hasn't seen Gavin in 43 days, her sons were off living their lives, her grandson was in rehab and nobody cared. She began to open her cabinets and smash all her dishes and drinkware on the floor. Chaos flooded her mind and she dumped over her plants and pushed her appliances off of the counters. By the time her rage was complete her hands and bare feet were bleeding and she was crying on the kitchen floor.Bradley sat in group therapy as if he hadn't ever been high. Somehow, he escaped the pains of with-drawals and had a great time. He listened to the stories of other people's rock bottom and made eyes at a girl in the far left of the circle. The Dr. observed his indifference and knew he was all the more in danger. Many juveniles don't experience with-drawals the same way as adults causing them to take their sobriety for granted. He was also noted for his eye contact with the young lady but would have a rude awakening if he thought they could engage in any intimate behavior. After the session ended, he struck up a conversation. Her name was Shelly and she also did Meth. He asked her how long she was in the program and she told him a couple weeks. He asked her where they were geographically and she told him. He said he wasn't allowed to make calls unattended and she said she was, He asked if she could call his friends and tell them where he was and to come get him the following evening at 10pm since it would be movie time. She agreed and completed the task. The following evening on New Year's Eve, Bradley escaped from Rehab.

After hosting the weekend after Christmas, Rhoda allowed her sister Vivian and brother-in-law Alex, to host New Year's Eve. Lexi, Paris and the kids stayed with her parents and Rhoda, Evans, Blake and the children went over for dinner. Ryan stayed in and told Blake he'd call her before midnight. The family had a ball playing games and watching holiday movies. Evans and Alex made their famous winter BBQ and everyone enjoyed their time together. They passed Paris's phone around to speak to his parents Pat and Parrish. Just when they thought the party was winding down Grandpa Rhodes and Mumzie decided to stop by. Rhoda hadn't seen them in weeks but was glad to see them. Blake and Lexi always chuckled thinking about the stuff Grandpa Rhodes got himself into by marrying Ryan and Paris's grandmother. They were both so feisty and did whatever they felt like doing. Rhodes caused a stir when he told them they decided to get out of the bed since they'd been loving for 3 days straight. Mumzie cracked up laughing while everyone else was traumatized. Rhoda told Blake that she and Ryan shouldn't be apart at midnight and to take the children back to the house and ask him to come over. Evans agreed. Blake called Ryan and invited him over so he drove over to bring in the new year with his family. Across Town, Joshua and Bella brought in the new year at home because Brielle had a cold. Freddie had dinner with the 4 of them, before falling asleep on the couch in their basement. Across town Gavin was preparing for Lilly's midnight show with no regard for walking away from his family. Only 2 miles from him was Victoria who was spending New Year's Eve alone for the first time in 45 years!

a new decade emerged filled with fresh promise and a hope for the future. Ryan awakened and turned to Blake and told her it was time for her and the children to come home. Blake faced him and asked what had changed. Ryan reminded her that they'd been doing well relating to one another and he felt good about it. Blake knew it was time to ask some questions. "Are you prepared to be home more often and reduce your travel itinerary? Are you going to share the responsibilities for our children and home?" Blake inquired. "Traveling to preach is how I support our lifestyle; you know my salary from the church doesn't cut it. What do you mean share the responsibilities for our children and home? You don't even work," Ryan said rudely. Blake's fire was stoked. "I will not step one foot in that house until you recognize what I bring to the table. I'm the glue that holds GLC together! You have no idea how many scandals and fires I've put out over the years." Blake said with tears in her eyes. "You sound like your damn momma but don't you worry, I start my new job on February 1st and you'll be home with your children since you only work on Sundays." Blake's heart was pounding. "Sundays, that's so lame you know it takes all week to prepare for Sundays," Ryan barked. "I can't tell," Blake responded. Ryan grew in offense and lashed out again. "Stop the drama Blake, just stop! What bag or shoe or piece of jewelry do I need to buy so you'll calm down and come home," Ryan taunted a second time. "Fool if you think for one second you can buy my silence and agreement you got me mistaken. I will never go back into that well decorated box you like to display me in," Blake responded. "I'm tired, it's old and I'm done being your spokeswoman and Stepford wife," Blake exclaimed. Ryan began getting dressed and sat on the bed to put on his shoes when the phone rang. It was Dr. France telling him that Bradley escaped from the treatment facility. Blake overheard the conversation and shook her head. Ryan thanked him for calling and turned to Blake, "you're not getting a job anywhere, you've got children to raise." Blake told him he would soon find out. Annoyed and ashamed, Ryan left the bedroom and headed toward the front door just as Rhoda and Evans returned from Vivian and Alex's house. Happy New Year, they said in unison noticing the troubled look on his face. Ryan returned the sentiment before Rhoda asked what was wrong. He told them that Bradley escaped from rehab and that Blake decided to get a job. They both told him to be safe looking for his son and walked to the closet to take off their coats. Ryan knew things were rapidly changing for his in-laws had never referred to Bradley in that manner. When Ryan sat in his car, he fought back tears. His phone rang again and it was his best friend Devin. The sound of his voice broke Ryan down to the ugly cry. He started his ignition so the call would transfer to his dashboard as he drove. He told Devin everything from the spitting incident to he and Blake's morning argument. Devin was a judge by profession and was very objective. He asked Ryan if he wanted his opinion. "Of course," Ryan responded. Devin took a deep breath, "you're wrong." Devin told Ryan had DJ spit in Zoe's face all bets were off. He reminded Ryan how much time he spent away from home, that even he himself told Ryan how Bradley's social media pages were disgusting. Devin also reminded Ryan and that he wouldn't be who or where he is without Blake. By the time their conversation ended, Ryan told Devin he would make things right. Devin told his best friend he would accept nothing less. The two men agreed to speak later in the week as Ryan entered his subdivision. Pulling into the garage, Ryan noticed that the door into the house was ajar. When he walked into the kitchen liquor bottles and drug paraphernalia were everywhere. Bradley had the nerve to celebrate the new year in the house with his friends. Ryan ran to his room to whoop him again but it was empty. He went from room to room looking for him. When he got to him and Blake's room, he noticed their bed was unmade and that the sheets were soiled. Ryan went off! He began swiping things off of their dresser and yelling at the top of his lungs. Just as he was pacing the floor, the doorbell rang. When he went to answer it, it was their neighbor Antoine Davis. "Hey Ryan, Happy New Year man. I just wanted you to know your son's guests backed a car into my mailbox early this morning and drove away without acknowledging the damage." Ryan apologized and told Antoine that he would take care of the cost. He thanked Ryan and told him it was being fixed later that day and he would bring over the bill for reimbursement. Ryan agreed and thanked him for telling him. "Bradley sure has changed," said Antoine before walking away. "He's on drugs," Ryan responded. Antoine turned around and saw Ryan's anguish. "You know better than anyone Rev, that God will get you through this," said Antoine before walking away. Ryan realized that church clichés are not comforting to hurting people and made a mental note to stop using them. He found no solace in those words but instead deep annoyance. Bradley was at Jenna's house with his friends getting high. He knew they had knocked down the Davis' mailbox and that he was wrong for having sex in his parent's bed so he needed an escape. The facility had proved to him that he could stop whenever he wanted. Everyone was cracking up and having fun. He got a text from Tia telling him to call her. He went into the bathroom to return her call so Jenna wouldn't know. When she answered, she told Bradley she was pregnant. He congratulated her and told Tia they would celebrate the next time they were together. She told him it was his. Bradley's high caused him to laugh uncontrollably. When he calmed down Tia said she was glad he was happy. Bradley told her it was great news and that he would see her soon. Just a few miles away, Victoria was cooking herself some breakfast when Barbara Edwards knocked on the door. Pleasantly surprised, Victoria opened the door to let her inside. Happy New Year, Victoria said but Barbara didn't respond. Barbara looked Victoria in the eye and told her that Bradley needed to stay away from Tia. When Victoria asked why, she told her that Tia had been introduced to drugs by Bradley and was now carrying his child. She informed Victoria that her and her husband were going to be taking Tia to an outpatient treatment program so the baby had a chance at a healthy life. Victoria grew angry and told Barbara to leave her house with those lies. "If he got her pregnant that's one thing but you will not accuse my grandson of doing drugs," Victoria exclaimed. Barbara replied, "I don't even know why I came here seeing as though Gavin doesn't even like you, I will talk to Blake and Ryan," before walking out of the door. Victoria was upset and called Gavin to tell him off for putting their business in the streets. When she called, the number was disconnected and Victoria immediately began to cry. How dare these people conspire to ruin her life, she thought. She was done with everything and everyone and vowed to make them all pay. Blake and the children sat eating breakfast when Evans walked into the kitchen. He was on his cell with his friend Jacob Nance. He told Blake that he wanted her to come the following day for her interview so she could begin working by January 20th. He was going to retire officially from a lengthy vacation and wanted her to be on the job before his last day on the 24th. Blake agreed and loved the idea of getting a sought-after government job without having to jump through hoops. Rhoda overheard the exchange and looked forward to Ryan's response when realizing how instrumental Blake was to his life. Blake asked her mother to keep an eye on the children while she went back to her and Ryan's home to get her black pantsuit. Rhoda agreed and Blake drove to the house she hadn't stepped foot in, for over a month. When Blake pulled into the driveway, she saw Ryan giving cash to Antoine Davis. When she stepped out of the car, she walked to the front door where the men were talking. "Happy New Year, First Lady," said Antoine. Blake returned the sentiment and asked how his family was doing. He filled her in on his wife's recent weight loss and the children's extracurricular activities. He also thanked Blake for the letter of recommendation she wrote, for his daughter to receive a scholarship to the dance academy. Ryan was again reminded how many people depended on his wife. Ryan assumed that Blake had come to make up and ended his conversation with Antoine. When Blake saw the trash bags lining their front door, she knew Bradley had been to the house. "You never took away his key?" Blake quizzed. Ryan took a deep breath never answering her question and told her that Bradley had sex in their bed. Blake shook her head as she walked up the staircase toward their master suite. Ryan followed as she keyed in the 10-digit code to unlock her second closet. Ryan never noticed the keypad on the door up until that point. He followed her inside only to realize his custom suits, jewelry and some of the children's belongings were also inside. "Let me guess, you had this installed because of him," said Ryan dryly. "We wouldn't have anything of value if I hadn't," said Blake. She placed a garment bag on the closet island and began to pull suits, blouses, and dresses from the racks. When Ryan asked what she was doing, Blake told him she had an interview the following day and would begin her new job earlier than expected. Ryan had no more fight in him and asked her about the position. He realized Evans knew before he told him and had orchestrated the whole thing. Ryan was tired of being a fool in his own marriage. He looked on in sadness as Blake packed more bags full of pumps, pantyhose and under garments. He knew she was going to accept the job and hoped it would wear her out so she'd quit. He had no problem taking care of his children but he didn't want his wife in the workforce. While Ryan brought Blake's bags to the car, he noticed a few neighbors looking his way. He shook his head knowing they were the cull de sac gossip mill. When Blake stepped outside behind him to carry a few bags to the truck, the group of women wished her a happy new year. Ryan became embarrassed by their presence and reentered the house. One of the women told Blake they hadn't see her in quite a while. Blake agreed and told the group that she was living with her parents until her and Ryan could work things out. Their quest for "hot tea" immediately brought conviction upon them. They were amazed by the woman of God's transparency. The group expected her to lie like everyone else and were sobered by her truth. Knowing their thoughts, Blake told them "pray for us" before going back inside with Ryan. Dismantled and defeated, each woman returned to her home to mind her own business. Once inside, Ryan asked Blake if she was returning to church. Blake told him no because she couldn't step one foot in GLC without being forced to work. "What if I told the congregation that you stepped down and will only be present as a worshipper," Ryan offered. "I would still be asked to do things by the members who feel entitled to my presence," Blake responded. "You know church folk think certain boundaries don't apply to them, especially those that tithe," Blake responded. Ryan had to admit that church folks were the worse at maintaining boundaries; yet they never seemed to do it wherever they drew a paycheck. Blake stood in her house looking at the chaotic place it had become. There were stains on her carpet and couch. Things were out of place and it smelled funky and stale. Ryan noticed how bad the house looked and followed Blake's eye around the room. "I'll buy you a new one," Ryan uttered softly. "When?" Blake quizzed excitedly. "When you find the one you want," Ryan offered. "What's my budget?" Blake asked. Ryan thought to himself and knew they had 2 years left on their 15-year mortgage so after the sale of the house they would walk away with half a million. "No more than $600k, I'd like our mortgage to be so low that the snowball stand can pay for it." Ryan stated. Blake agreed. Their snowball stand profited about $5k per month from April-September. That would turn out to be $2500.00 each month for the year. That was surely enough to finance $100k of the new house. The Hairstons' had learned to make their assets pay for their expenses. They also knew the value of having a mortgage for tax purposes. Blake told Ryan she would start looking that evening and Ryan told her he would assume nothing less. They laughed before sharing a passionate kiss and Ryan walked Blake to her truck.

When Ryan stepped back into the house, he was exhausted. How could the first day of a new year and decade begin so awfully. His family was coming undone at the seams and his wife no longer resided under his roof. He looked in the refrigerator only to find it bare and decided to order delivery. Ryan despised the idea of random people delivering his food but he was hungry and too tired to drive. He placed and paid for his food with enough for his next 2 meals. He laid on the couch and turned on the tv above the fireplace. He decided to watch the sports channel. When the house phone rang, he knew it had to be important so he walked to the kitchen to grab the phone. It was Prophet Tevin. Yet again Ryan felt misty eyed as he did when Devin called. Tevin didn't speak with his usual

booming voice rather subdued and restrained. Ryan immediately knew something was wrong. Tevin made small talk and
wished him a happy new year. When Ryan asked what was
wrong, PT began to weep. With his heart sinking in anticipa-
tion, Ryan listened intently. Tevin told Ryan that Gabrielle had
stage 4 breast cancer and that it has already spread to other
organs. Ryan couldn't believe his ears. Tevin continued that
they'd only found out 22 days prior and already she was in and
out of consciousness. Ryan wept with him. "How am I a
prophet of God yet I had no knowledge of my wife's decaying
health?" Tevin inquired. Ryan sat in silence with tears
streaming down his face. Tevin spoke about his life on the road
ministering to everyone else while his wife raised Timothy and
Tiffany, by herself. He spoke about his traveling men's conference and how he saw miracles in the lives of others. Ryan
remembered it was Tevin's Dallas men's conference where he
found out about Bradley. Tevin spoke about how they met, fell
in love, and got married. Ryan continued to listen as he too
thought about his high school sweetheart Blake Kensington.
Tevin spoke about the true cost of ministry and Ryan began to
rock back and forth. He added up the sacrifice, pain, struggle,
rumors, court cases, articles, news stories, blog posts, lack of
privacy, gossip, slander, misunderstandings, lies, investigations,
accusations, and betrayals. The phrase quietly left Tevin's lips
"serving the ungrateful costs way too much." Ryan felt that
statement in his soul. For the following 5 hours and 3 cordless
phones later, the 2 friends vowed to have a life and that more
abundantly; because tomorrow wasn't promised. Unable to take
one more thing, Ryan opened the front door to grab the food
that spent hours on the stairs. He forced himself to eat before
taking a shower and falling asleep.

The following morning Blake arrived at the address she was
given on Embassy Row. Clad in her black cashmere coat, black
St. John pantsuit, black leather Jimmy Choo stilettos and

carrying a matte black Lady Dior bag she mounted the stairs and entered the building. After the checkpoint she was given a badge in exchange for her driver's license and escorted to a large hallway filled with elevator doors. She asked a gentleman in the hallway which set of elevators led to the suite she was looking for because they had no buttons and only a keyhole. He instructed her around the corner to the visitor's elevator and said an operator would be there. When she arrived at the correct place, the operator greeted her and she was whisked to the 7th floor of the building. Once off, she turned left and entered a set of double glass doors. When the receptionist greeted her, she escorted Blake to a conference room to wait for Mr. Nance and his colleague Carla Sanders. When the 2 of them entered the room, Blake stood up to meet them and realized he was the man who gave her directions downstairs. Jacob told Blake that he and her father went way back to their time in Frankfurt, Germany. He also knew her brothers who served with his son. The interview began as Blake was asked some odd questions. She answered them truthfully but wondered if she answered them correctly. When Carla excused herself, Jacob assured Blake she was doing fine but the sensitive nature of the job required the odd questions. He told her that her background check had been expedited and that he expected to have it within a week. Blake would be required to train for 3 months before actually performing the job but would be paid. He informed her that they were paid twice per month on the 15th and 30th no matter what day it fell on. Jacob also informed her that her training salary would be $40/hr. but would advance to $50 once she passed all her assessments. Mr. Nance had Blake fill out her forms and Carla gave her a set of badges for the parking lot, office door and elevator. She informed Blake that they wouldn't be active until the morning of the 20th and that they are only enabled between 7am and 4pm. Her training shift would be from 7:00am -3pm Monday through Friday. They were given an hour of paid lunch and her day would include an hour of shadowing a senior official. Blake thanked Mr. Nance and Carla for their time before being given an entirely different address to report to on the first day. Blake made her way down through the lobby before retrieving her license in exchange for the badge and walked back to her car. Realizing she was afraid of what the future held, she decided she needed the reassurance of her man. She called Ryan as she pulled out of the lot and turned onto Massachusetts Avenue. The phone went to voicemail. When she hung up, she thought about how much their lives were going to change with her working outside the home. Together they had built a house for God but something inside of Blake felt the tide changing. She loved serving people especially empowering other women but she needed something for herself. The price of ministry had taken its toll on their marriage and family and Blake was tired of paying the cost. She desired a more traditional life. Just then she decided to call her friend Ardena who always made her feel better at times like this. When Ardena answered Blake was comforted by her voice. Always full of wisdom Blake asked Ardena if they could meet during the week for lunch. She agreed and the two friends would sit and talk the following day. Blake was so excited and her anxiety disappeared. As she pulled onto the ramp to head back to Maryland, Ryan returned her call. Blake was so thrilled to hear his voice. Ryan asked if she could stop by and she agreed. His voice was weak and Blake grew concerned. Ryan asked her to bring him something to eat and she agreed before he ended the call. Blake reached the exit to their house and stopped by a soul food spot to order his meal. She hadn't cooked for him in months and made a mental note to start making sure he eats. She placed an order for smothered beef tips, rice and cabbage. She also bought him a half n' half and a slice of chocolate cake. She decided to get herself a slice as well. When she walked back to her truck, she noticed Gavin's car at the light. She hadn't seen her father-in-law since October. She needed to log into the church records and get Lilly's address to pay him a visit, she thought. When Blake arrived at the house she pulled into the garage and entered the house through the kitchen. Ryan was laying on the couch talking on the phone. She washed her hands and made his plate, transferring the food into real dishes. When she approached him with the serving tray, she could tell he'd been crying. He asked the person he was speaking to if he could call him back because she had brought him something to eat. He said a few okays before he offered to call the person back and ended the call. Ryan looked at Blake in her suit and asked how her interview went, she told him it was weird and that she was afraid of what working would mean. He shook his head in agreement before tasting his food. Ryan turned to Blake and told her they had to fly to Atlanta the following week. When she asked why, he fought back tears while telling her that Gabrielle Coleman passed away in the middle of the night. Blake's body went numb! Gabby was too young and beautiful to die, Blake thought. Ryan told her about Gabby's diagnosis just 23 days ago. Blake wept for her children losing their mom and Ryan wept for Tevin losing his wife. Ryan asked Blake to make their travel arrangements and to book their hotel but she crawled across the couch into his arms and cried. Ryan held his wife as she wept. Both knew their pain was deeper than Gabby's loss. While lying in her husband's arms Blake uttered the timely words that had penetrated his soul when Tevin spoke them similarly, "life in the public eye is too expensive. I just want us to be happy again." Blakes words pierced Ryan just as Tevin's did. He didn't know exactly what the future held but it had to be different. Hours later, Blake made their travel arrangements while Ryan got some sleep. She could see the stress on his face as he slept. While sitting in Ryan's home office she accessed the church data base and wrote down Lilly's last known address.

The family was falling apart and Gavin was nowhere to be found. Though Ryan and Joshua are grown men they still needed their father and though she had Evans, she needed Gavin too. Later that evening when Blake was about to leave, Bradley walked in the front door. Annoyed that her husband hadn't changed the locks she said nothing to upset him. Ryan had slept but not rested and had no strength to argue or fight with him. Blake was amazed by his appearance. Though he was only 17 he looked like a 30-year-old. His hair was overgrown and his skin was ashy and filthy. He looked like he rolled out of a trash can and his missing teeth didn't help. "Hey Dad. Hey Blake." Bradley said awkwardly, while walking to his room. Ryan's heart broke into pieces hearing Bradley call her by her first name. Blake told him months prior that he stopped calling her Mom but hearing it with his own ears was devastating. Ryan walked Blake to the garage and kissed his wife goodbye. Ryan stood in the frigid driveway as Blake drove down the street honking her horn at the corner. Realizing who she was honking to, he also waved as Joshua, Bella and the kids, Brielle, and Joshua Jr., drove past on their way home. Ryan went back in the house to find Bradley eating the rest of his food. Instead of fighting, arguing, or yelling, Ryan sat beside him and ate his chocolate cake before Bradley could. Ryan asked him how he's been and Bradley told him he was sick. He told his father that his stomach has been upset and that he's been getting headaches. Ryan offered to take him to the doctor and he declined. When Ryan asked him what his plans were since he'd be 18 this summer, Bradley said he was going to travel and see the world. Ryan knew the boy didn't have a dime to his name but humored his drug addicted son. "Where are you going?" Ryan asked. "Miami" Bradley replied. Ryan always heard that drugs reduce a person's brain cells but being a world traveler to Miami was worse than he expected. That evening Ryan made Bradley take a shower and wash his hair. Afterwards they sat in the living room watching movies while Ryan searched for a glimpse of the son he loved so dearly. As if he could hear the cry of his father's heart, Bradley brought up the day they met and how much he missed Brooke's late grandmother Granny Mae. Ryan agreed that she was the best. He asked Bradley if he missed his mother and Bradley told Ryan that he didn't know Brooke anymore and that she was too concerned with men, Davina and Quest. Ryan knew Bradley was referring to Brooke's reality star days on *Football Fiancés*. Ryan hated the show himself and remembered the legal actions he had to take to shut down Brooke's storyline. He also recounted the day Blake discovered Brooke with her 2 youngest children at a shelter in St. Louis. Rejecting the opportunity to join the Brooke Bash, Ryan reminded Bradley that his mother loves him and wants to see him get better. Ryan asked Bradley what he did wrong as a father. Bradley told him "You put church and god stuff before me." Ryan apologized. Bradley said okay. Ryan asked Bradley what he needed to do for him to get well and Bradley told him nothing. "Just take care of your wife and your kids," Bradley lashed back. "You are one of my kids," Ryan expressed. "Yeah but Blake raised me," Bradley responded. "Then why the disrespect?" Ryan asked. "She doesn't let me do anything but sit in that stupid church," Bradley answered. Ryan knew there were plenty of PKs' who never ended up on drugs but took responsibility for always being on the road. It was there that he failed his family. Ryan told Bradley that he loved him and was so sorry for hurting him. Bradley appreciated his father's admittance and asked for a hug. Ryan obliged and felt the racing heart of his first-born son. Ryan knew it wasn't normal for someone's heart to beat that fast at rest. Tears streamed from his tired eyes giving way to a full-blown migraine. Bradley's emaciated body was a far cry from how he looked just months ago. Ryan didn't know if or when he would get his son back but he was certainly going to try. Feeling the trickle of his father's tears down the side of his face made Bradley believe he was crying too. The following afternoon Blake walked into Fig and Olive to meet Ardena for lunch. Sitting at the table waiting for her arrival. Ardena stood to greet her. They hugged so tight and were thrilled to see each other. Blake could smell the Emerald Reign perfume Ardena was wearing and she could smell Blake's fragrance of the day *Cassili*. Both women wore grey head to toe and laughed how fashionable minds think alike. Both ladies chose the F&O Burger with a Pellegrino. The two friends laid it all on the table. Ardena was saddened that Blake was forced out of her home. They shared everything from friendships to mothers-in-law. Blake was floored when Ardena shared about her and her family's experiences within the church. She and Ryan told Ardena and JT for years to take the extra drive to GLC. Blake's mouth was wide open. They both agreed that most people don't go into ministry planning on being who they become. Blake was encouraged. There are very few women she can just be herself with and they are Lexi, Ardena and her masseuse Kari. Ardena gave Blake 6 months to get her marriage and family back on track with time to settle into a new home. Blake gave Ardena 3 months to change her perception about her day job. The women laughed when talking about old times and were hopeful about the future. They both decided to have dessert and ordered the apple tarts. After lunch they walked over to the City Center Valet to get their vehicles. In true Ardena fashion she pulled out a gift bag and handed it to Blake. Always prepared, Blake pulled out a card and handed it to Ardena. Their automobiles arrived at the same time otherwise the first person to get her car, would wait with the other. They hugged goodbye as Ardena got into her Lincoln Aviator and Blake into her Bentayga. They were so much alike it was often creepy to their spouses. Later that evening when Blake opened her gift, it was the large bottle of *Delina Exclusif* perfume, which she loved instantly. Nia and Ardena were the best at buying Blake perfume. Miles away when Ardena opened her card it was a gift card to Jo Malone. Blake knew her so well.

Ryan and Blake landed at Hartsfield-Jackson Atlanta International Airport. It was the day before Gabby's funeral but her wake would be that evening. The couple held hands as they rode the escalator to the train. When they got off at the baggage claim they decided to eat at their hotel before settling into their room. When they received their luggage a car service was waiting for them per Tevin's insistence. Tevin's church secretary was also with the driver to assist them over the weekend. Ryan was blown away that in his loss Tevin was still concerned about them. Linda Fanning had been with Tevin and Gabby before they had a physical location. She asked the Hairstons' if they needed to stop anywhere before checking in. Ryan told her no. When they arrived at the Four Seasons, Linda told the couple she would return for them at 5pm sharp as Tevin requested that they sit with him and the children. Ryan was floored but agreed. It was 10am and Ryan just wanted some food, another shower, and the bed. Once they were settled in their room, they ordered room service. Ryan took a shower first just in case the food came. While Blake dried off from her shower the food had just arrived. Blake just threw on her bathrobe so she could eat while the food was hot. Ryan ate his food and immediately got into bed for a nap. When Blake took off her robe to finish her skincare regiment Ryan miraculously caught a second wind. When she felt his eyes burning a hole in her back, she turned around to see him holding her chocolate candy bar. The following morning Blake was numb standing over Gabby's body. She was too young, too vibrant, and too beautiful to be inside of a coffin. Her mind couldn't comprehend the thought of Timothy and Tiffany growing up without her. Life changes so fast, she thought. Blake stood at the casket so long that dozens of people had come and gone. Ryan sat on the front row with Tevin, the children, and Gabby's parents. He wondered what Blake was thinking or feeling she'd been standing there so long. Tevin looked over at Ryan and told him to go get her. Ryan gently walked up behind her and wrapped his arms around her waist. The floodgates opened and Blake came undone. The way she cried sent everyone into deep grief. As if a dominos had fallen, row by row people were weeping in agony with her. Ryan had to drag Blake to her seat. Even Tevin knew Blake's agony wasn't just about Gabby. He perceived that she was mourning the life she once knew. He also felt her anxiety to step into an uncertain future. He understood. How was he supposed to rear a teenaged daughter through hormonal shifts and horrible boys? How would he nurture his son with the wisdom of a woman...he couldn't? Tevin's uncle Percy led Gabby's service. Ryan was blown away during Tevin's words about his wife. His strength, his regret. There wasn't a dry eye in the house when Tevin shared with all in attendance that within 4 days of Gabby's diagnosis, she had bought and wrapped birthday and Christmas gifts for their children all the way up to their 30th birthday. At just 12 years old they would have 18 years' worth of their mother's earthly expressions of love. She put on her signature lipstick and kissed 2 hankies, one for each of their wedding days. Tevin told his children she would always be with them as they are each made from half of her and half of him. Gabby's mother was in agony. She couldn't bare it and blacked out. Without panic or excitement Tevin asked Linda to dial 911. He knew she would be okay. The paramedics came and ushered her to a local hospital. Gabby's sister and niece went with her as her father refused to leave. Tevin shared with the family that though he made mistakes he didn't have time to repair he was so thankful that his friend Ryan would. Ryan cried silently and shook his head in agreement that he would make things right for his family. During the repass Tevin walked from table to table greeting all who came.

The kids were right beside him not wanting him to leave them. They followed him around for over an hour until his mother made him sit down and eat. Ryan pushed his food around his plate as some of their colleagues in ministry spoke about work. Ryan could care less about the needs of the ministry and was annoyed by their insensitivity. Blake sat beside him rocking in her chair. The intercessors were praying for her from their respective seats. Tevin's mother couldn't take it anymore and walked up to Blake and took her up in her arms and rocked her. She could feel the pain and disappointment in Blakes heart. When Tevin sat beside Ryan to eat his food, his family made sure nobody approached him. The children on the other side of him, agreed to eat as well. Ryan looked at Tiffany and thought about Rayne. He certainly loved his sons but he vowed to one day see the excitement for his presence back in her eyes. That evening the couple went over Tevin and Gabby's house with a small group of the family. Blake laid down in the guestroom while Tevin and Ryan talked in the basement. Tevin's mom washed clothes and his sisters cleaned the house. Tevin was the only boy in his family and they knew he needed their help. He was grateful to come from a large family and to still have his parents for the days ahead. The following day, Blake and Ryan went to Tevin and Gabby's for brunch before their early evening flight back to Maryland. Momma Coleman gave Blake her number as Tevin's sister Tina. By the time the Hairston's made it to the Delta Sky lounge they were drained. When they entered Evans and Rhoda's house the children ran up to greet them. When Ryan saw the happiness in Rayne's face, he couldn't help but to cry. It was just under a week before Blake would start her new job with the federal government. Though she was nervous she decided she would still show up. As she pulled up in front of Lilly's house, she didn't know what to expect. Taking a deep breath, she walked up to the door and rang the bell. Gavin answered the door in shock. "Hey Dad, can we talk?" Blake asked. Gavin agreed and let her in but looked out the door behind her to see if anyone was with her. When Lilly saw Blake, she immediately buttoned her shirt and pretended to fix her hair. Though she had a ball with Gavin she wasn't expecting her pastor's wife to walk into her home. Blake spoke and Lilly returned the sentiment feeling embarrassed and ashamed. Blake thought it was interesting that Lilly was shy around the pastor's wife but not the pastor's father. Gavin offered her a seat and sat beside her. Blake told Gavin everything without ever acknowledging how she knew where to find him. He knew Freddie and Evans didn't give him up. Confused and embarrassed himself he comforted his daughter the best way he could. When she mentioned Victoria, Gavin became disgusted and told Blake he was never going back. After a few hours of catching up, Blake thanked Gavin for listening and said she'd be back soon. Gavin gave Blake his number and told her to call first. Miles away, Ryan sat in his office in GLC when Jason his worship leader, knocked on the door. Ryan motioned for him to come in and Jason sat down. When Ryan asked Jason, what brought him in today, he told Ryan he received the call to pastor. Ryan congratulated him. I want to plant a church and I was hoping I'd have your blessing to plant a second location of GLC. Ryan loves people like Jason who walk right in and lay it all out on the table. He hates sitting with people for hours who fail to say what they really want. Jason was shocked to hear Ryan say, "You don't need to plant GLC 2 when you can have GLC." "Come again," said Jason. "I'll be stepping down soon and my good friend Prophet Tevin Coleman told me that my successor would be revealed to me this week." Ryan said enthusiastically. Ryan told Jason to get a pad and a pen so they could work out the transition plan. "You're too happy, should I be afraid?" Jason asked. "I don't know if *you* should be afraid, but *I* will never hold another office in the church again," Ryan said assuredly. For the next five hours the mentor and mentee hammered out a plan that would be offered to the congregants in phases. When they were finished, Jason asked if he was being punked. Ryan reminded Jason that he was minding his black owned business, when Jason knocked on the door. He agreed and looked at Ryan as if he still didn't believe it. "How can I further assist you Pastor Kemp?" Ryan asked. "I'm just taken aback because this was so easy," Jason responded. "The difficulty in ministry doesn't come in the preparation, it comes with the people. You're about to become a moving target for what *you* say *you* believe." Ryan explained. "You were prepared for this years ago when your name was scandalized around the globe." Ryan assured him. Jason took a deep breath and remembered the dark days of his past. He overcame one of the biggest scandals in church history, though gossip spread faster than apologies. "One last thing," Jason said to Ryan. "I'm not preaching colonized Christianity. I'm using the scriptures to illustrate principles that will lead people away from believing in a spooky version of God, so they'll begin to do for themselves." Jason finished. Ryan smiled knowing he was leaving GLC in capable hands. "I would expect nothing less." Ryan responded. Ryan was so proud of Jason. He knew the average parishioner sits in wait of a God who will mysteriously perform outcomes without input. The spin around 3 times and high five your neighbor message was so destructive. He's watched countless people place money they didn't have on altars in hopes of financial breakthroughs after weeks of fasting and hours of praying. Ryan never played those games with God's people. He and Blake saved so much money because of some people's generosity, that they were able to invest well. The couple owned real estate, rental properties, retail establishments and generated income from teaching online courses. Though he hadn't confirmed to Blake that it was time to move on, Ryan planned to return to his first love, architecture. He and Elder Lawson always joked that Ryan should be the 3rd partner at *Taylor Made*.

Lawson owned an architectural firm with his partner Taylor Vance. Lawson's last name is Taylor and Ryan's middle name is Taylor. Ryan decided to call Lawson. When Lawson answered Ryan spoke "This is a covert mission. Once the call disconnects, you will speak nothing of it." Ryan said in a robotic voice. "Understood" responded Lawson fighting back a hearty laugh. "How much to buy in at 1/3?" Ryan inquired in his normal voice." Excited about what this would mean for the firm, Lawson sat up in his chair and stopped laughing. "2.3" Lawson said hoping this was his dream come true. "It will arrive Wednesday. Send the paperwork to my attorney, Devonshire Braxton dbraxtonesq@kingmail.com. Lawson agreed and the call was over. Lawson went over to Taylor's office to tell him the secret news. Taylor was so excited because Ryan bought so much expertise to the table that were outside of, he and Lawson's expertise. It took years to convince him but it was right on time! They immediately called the firm's business attorney, Anedra Henson to draw up the papers and send them to Devin. Ryan was hopeful when he hung up the phone. It was time to get his house in order. He would return to secular life and Jason would lead the church into her brightest hour. He had to get Blake back home and out of the workforce as soon as possible, see the spark back in the twins' eyes, make Royce feel secure, sell the house, buy a new house and get Bradley off the dime. The task was large but it had to be done.

4

SELF CARE

*B*lake pulled up to the address she had just been provided with an hour prior and parked in the spot with her ID number on it. Assuming she'd have to drive to D.C. every morning, she was shocked to find a federal building complex just 15 minutes from the new house she fell in love with in Mitchellville, Maryland. When she got out of her truck, she was greeted by a security guard who looked more like a soldier ready for war. He led her to a set of glass doors and told her to scan and rescan her badge until she arrived at the reception area. Blake walked through 3 security doors before entering a sprawling office suite with a hug reception area. Before she could tell the receptionist who she was, Carla walked up to greet her. Carla introduced Blake to the receptionist before escorting Blake to her desk. Blake's desk was located in a quiet room where the 11 researchers she would lead were working. Blake would have full view of all 11 workers and would see anyone long before they approached her desk. There were no windows in the research area but they had their own restrooms, lounge, and café. Carla gave Blake a set of keys to all the cabinets and drawers attached to her Executive style desk.

Her desk was an iMac with double monitors. She also had a large leather office chair with massage and heat settings. Adjacent to her desk was a small closet with a bar to hang her coat, handbag, and a receptacle for an umbrella. Carla encouraged Blake to lock her personal items inside the closet and follow her. Blake was introduced to her staff which consisted of 10 women and one man. The women sized Blake up as they pretended to smile. Noticing the quality of her Balmain suit and Saint Lauren heels, they immediately wrote her off as uppity and untrustworthy. The only man on her staff, Marvin, loved it. He was totally into fashion and gave Blake a loud "Yeassss Hunty!" which made her smile. As Carla led Blake away on a tour and greeting session, Marvin could be heard saying "Miss Blake is here to show ya'll heauxs how it's done. Did ya'll see those wedding rings? Slay B."Carla took Blake everywhere! Department by department. Her eyes widened as she saw the full-on cafeteria that made gourmet food. They had a pharmacy, a dry cleaner, an optician, and a general store. While in the web development department she was introduced to the project manager, Kelvin Franklin. When Kelvin saw Blake, he couldn't believe his eyes. Carla told Blake that she and Kelvin would work closely together since many of his department's developments are based on her department's research. Half of Blake's staff works in policy and the other half works in intelligence. Blake noticed how handsome Kelvin was and made sure not to stare. Kelvin smirked when he saw Blake's rings. He thought to himself that things should liven up, real soon. He told Blake it was a pleasure to meet her and she responded, likewise. It was already noon by the time Carla's tour ended. She and Blake stopped in the cafeteria to get something to eat. They could order anything they wanted and it would be reconciled by an account that would subtract it from their pay or be paid directly to the account. Because Blake was in leadership, her meals and snacks were included in her bene-

fits package. There was so much to choose from. Blake fought
the urge to order crab cakes and decided to order a garden
salad topped with chicken salad. "Don't be shy, we get our grub
on around here," said Kelvin from behind. Blake turned around
and laughed dryly as Kelvin winked his eye. Blake put her salad
on her tray, grabbed a Pellegrino and walked away. She could
feel Kelvin's eyes follow her to the table where Carla was
waiting for her. Carla had cream of crab soup and some crusty
bread. She told Blake it was okay to order food at the end of the
day to take home. "Many nights, I grab a soup or stir-fry on my
way out to eat for dinner." Blake thanked her for the information but had no intention of making it a habit. She has an entire
family to feed unlike someone who only has themselves. It was
2 o'clock before Blake returned to her desk. Her staff's shift
ends at 2:30 and hers ends at 3:00. During lunch Carla told
Blake that her training class wasn't necessary but that she'd just
shadow a senior official for a few weeks. Blake was confused
but decided to go with the flow. While sitting at her desk, each
staff member placed a flash-drive in the slot of a locked box at
her desk before leaving. As they were leaving, Kelvin
approached Blake with a stack of folders. He pulled up a chair
opposite her and placed the files on her desk. "I know you're
about to leave but Carla assigned you to shadow me. I used to
have your job in the previous building before the person you
just replaced," said Kelvin. Blake listened as he explained what
her actual job duties were and why each worker had to turn in
their flash drive every day. Because of the sensitive nature of the
job they were to start each day with a new flash drive and take
nothing home. Kelvin's department would receive the flash
drives after Blake opens them to retrieve the data necessary to
report specific findings. In addition to Blake's report she was
also responsible for researching classified documents and
report her findings to her superiors. There would be weekly
briefings on Tuesdays and Thursdays with her superiors and

she'd conduct a weekly meeting on Fridays with her own staff. Kelvin gave Blake a policy book that she was allowed to study at home but it had to come back with her each day. Blake asked Kelvin if she had to be off the lot by 4 as she was told in her interview? He told her yes but only for the 90 days of her training period. Kelvin asked Blake if she knew how to get back to her car. She admitted that she didn't so he volunteered to show her the fastest way there. During their walk Blake learned that her parking spot wasn't in the main lot. She parked in the lot with everyone who was over a staff. When they arrived at the door Blake had entered that morning, the same security guard was still there. Blake thanked Kelvin for walking her to the glass doors and exited toward the parking lot. Kelvin was blown away to see her climb into a Bentley. He walked back to his office thinking Blake was no average woman. Excited and relieved that her first day of working a job in over a decade, was under her belt. Blake called Rhoda to tell her it wasn't that bad. Rhoda was excited and told Blake she was making her favorite crab cakes for dinner. Before hanging up she could hear the children coming into the house from school. Evans picked them up on Mondays and they sounded like a rowdy bunch of sugar consumers. Rhoda ended the call with Blake after noticing cookie crumbs on Royce's face. Blake shook her head and told her mom she would see them soon. Evans always let the children punk him before dinner. She knew her mother was at home fussing. A few moments later, Ryan called to ask how her first day went. Blake smiled as her husband quizzed her about her day. He hadn't asked in so long. She spared the tiny details but gave him the cliff's notes version of her day. He told her he'd see her in a couple hours for Rhoda's famous crab cakes. She agreed and smiled before disconnecting the call. By the time she pulled up into the Evans' driveway she received calls from Lexi, Ardena and Devin's wife Zoe. After dinner, Ryan went back into Blake's bedroom to talk and Royce followed behind them. Blake showed Ryan the house she found in a gated community on a real time realty website. It was a 5-bedroom 4.5 bath home with all their preferred features. Blake required a huge island with room for seating and a sink, sperate glass surround shower and soaker tub in the master and a loft. Ryan required a finished basement, theater room, large back-yard for an outdoor kitchen and a separate office space. Reign and Ryan Jr. would have separate bathrooms and Royce would have a small enclave in his room for a play area. The house was $675 but Ryan was willing to overlook the extra money to have a turnkey home. Blake had no desire to change any of the fixtures, flooring or cabinets which made Ryan happy. The home was exactly her taste and style. He did know that she expected all new furniture but thankfully the only construction necessary was his outdoor kitchen. Ryan dialed their broker to set up a walk through and was set up for 5 o'clock the following day. Ryan was annoyed to see the house so late in the day but Blake had a job. "You like obligating yourself to these time constraints?" Ryan mocked. "I love it," Blake snapped back. Ryan rolled his eyes and remembered what Grandad Sands told him. Ryan secretly hoped the job would wear Blake down so she'd want to quit. He decided not to tell her he was stepping down as Senior Pastor or that he was returning to architecture. He decided to use it as a trump card for later. He knew he was wrong but she knew she didn't need a job. The following morning Blake arrived at work in a good mood. She couldn't wait to see her new house. She called her prayer warriors to agree in prayer that nobody would buy it from underneath them. She would've wanted to see the house that morning as well but she learned from Ryan how to stick to her decisions no matter how they affected everyone else. She was serving him a plate of humble pie from his recipe book. "Good morning everyone" she spoke, followed by a mix of responses. A few women scoffed, most said good morning and a "yeassss boss lady" came from Marvin. Taking note of the wardrobe culture during her tour with Carla, Blake knew it was acceptable to wear skirts and dresses. She wore a midi length pleated A line skirt in forest green leather, with a black chiffon bow blouse and forest green blazer. To top it off she wore her long Chanel necklace, Rolex, Cartier love bangles and black suede Tom Ford booties. Before she reached her desk, Marvin exclaimed "I smell that Baccarat boss lady." Blake turned back and smiled. Marvin was sure to be the best part of her days. Once she put her things away, Blake logged into her work email. She had a meeting from 8:00am to 11:00am. While answering a few emails from some of her peers who she met the day before, Kelvin arrived at her desk. Blake said good morning and noticed his fresh shape up and new clothes. They still had the new clothes smell though he was wearing cologne. Blake knew she inspired his new look and laughed within herself. "Good morning, we have a busy day ahead of us," Kelvin explained. Blake agreed mentioning the 3-hour meeting. He told Blake the meeting was every bit of 3 hours every time and to bring a snack if she didn't want to be served the heaps of sugar on the refreshment table. It's a carb lover's dream in these meetings: Bagels, donuts, pastry and juice. They do have herbal teas and coffee as well. Blake planned to grab some nuts and a bottled water. For the following forty minutes before heading to the meeting, Kelvin went over some of the policies and procedures. Blake listened intently and asked questions for clarity when necessary. On their way to the board room Blake picked up some nuts and water from the café and Kelvin picked up a protein bar. When they got on the elevator, he asked how long she's been married. "Almost 15 years," Blake responded. "Kids?" Kelvin asked. "A stepson and 3 natural children," Blake said before the doors opened. "He's a lucky man," Kelvin responded. Usually responding with the cliché "we're not lucky we're blessed" Blake chose instead; "He sure is!" The meeting was a hoot.

Blake couldn't believe the hilarity that existed so high up in the government structure. Judging solely off behavior she wondered how most of them earned their titles and jobs. In addition to the comedy she learned so much! She took great notes knowing the things she was learning transcended her position and was "free game" for a prosperous life. The average person had no idea what was available to them. She always knew people perished for a lack of knowledge but didn't realize how much information was purposely withheld from the masses. After the meeting, Blake decided to grab something to eat before shadowing Kelvin for the rest of the day. He invited himself to join her and she agreed. Blake decided to order soup since Carla's looked so good the day before. She settled on the chicken and wild rice soup and a pumpkin cheesecake muffin. Kelvin waved her down at a table in the corner. Blake joined him and began to eat her food. While the two colleagues were making small talk, Kelvin recited a Chris Rock joke causing Blake to laugh heartily. When her phone rang, she answered it still smiling. When she said hello, Ryan said he hopes it was him who put that smile on her face. She said it was. Kelvin got up from the table and told Blake he'll be right back. Ryan hearing his voice asked, "who is that?" Blake informed him it was her colleague Kelvin who would be training her for the next 3 months. Ryan grew annoyed. "What's his last name?" Ryan quizzed. "I forgot," Blake responded. Ryan told her to find out by the end of the day. Blake was amused that he was jealous. Remembering what grandad said, Ryan pretended that it didn't bother him and told Blake he was thinking of her and to enjoy the rest of her workday. Blake thanked him and disconnected the call. For the remainder of the day, Blake grew anxious about her new home and couldn't wait to see it. At the end of the day, Blake hurried to gather her things. She and Ryan agreed to go in the same car so she made her way to their house. When she pulled into the driveway, Ryan exited the front door and motioned for her to get in the passenger seat. Blake walked around the car kissing him as they walked past one another. When she got back into the car, Ryan adjusted the seat and plugged the address into the navigation system. With after work traffic and current conditions, they would arrive exactly at 5 o'clock. Ryan was still annoyed by the time slot but backed out of the driveway. He told his wife she looked beautiful and looked her over. "What's his last name?" Ryan asked again. Not wanting to argue, Blake responded "Franklin" with a dismissive tone. Ryan put on some music and tried to enjoy their alone time but wanted to call his government connect about Kelvin. By divine intervention, the Hairstons' arrived at the house at 4:55pm. Their broker was parked out front and got out of his car when they pulled into the driveway. Gregory was one of the countless success stories from Ryan's mentoring group. He greeted the couple and used the keypad to enter the house. The entryway of the 4,500 square foot home was a showstopper. As they walked from room to room, they were convinced it was where they belonged. Ryan told Gregory to put in an offer at $665k. He agreed and stepped away from the couple to call the realtor selling the property while simultaneously faxing the offer already typed up with only the dollar amount to add before submitting. While they were alone, Ryan backed Blake into the glass surround shower and picked her up. With his hands gripping her butt and her legs around his waist, he told her he couldn't wait to enjoy her against the wall. Blake started giggling as Ryan simulated his plans. They didn't notice Gregory's return so he pretended to clear his throat "eh em." "Didn't your parents teach you to knock boy?" Ryan teased. "With all due respect, it's not every day you see your Pastor and First lady planning the get down" Gregory responded. Ryan loved greasy talk and started to respond but didn't want Blake to be mortified. They toured the house a second and a third time. Before leaving, Ryan thanked Gregory and Blake hugged him. When they got back into the car, Ryan asked Blake to spend the night with him. Blake reminded him that Bradley had been in their bed with God knows who and Ryan remembered. He's been sleeping on the couch ever since. Blake told him to spend the night with her but he declined. "I don't want to have sex with my wife at her momma and daddy's house all the time," Ryan said boldly. "Let's get a room," Ryan suggested. "Okay but you'll have to bring me to work tomorrow," Blake agreed. About to blow a fuse and act a fool, he remembered what grandad Sands said; Ryan swallowed his pride and drove in silence toward The Four Seasons. Blake needed to call Rhoda to tell her she would be out with Ryan for the night. Ryan felt convicted because the children hadn't seen her all day and agreed to go to her parent's house. "May I point out yet again, that your job doesn't work for our family," Ryan said as calmly as he could. "I understand but I have to do this for me," Blake responded. "How so?" Ryan inquired. "I want my own money and time to do what I want to do. All I've done for the past 10 years is serve everyone else's needs." Blake responded sincerely. Ryan knew she was right and knew he had to devise a way for Blake to earn a salary and have more time for herself. "How much do they pay you?" Ryan asked. "$40/hr. for 90 days, then $50 moving forward," Blake answered. Ryan did the math in his head "That's over $91k a year," he exclaimed. "The first year, but over $100k with a full year of non-training pay," Blake explained. "I'm claiming the kids too," said Blake. "Girl I almost cussed, no you're not," Ryan exclaimed. "You better claim zero," he added. "No way, the tax man will eat me to shreds." Blake exclaimed. "Woman, the tax man will be the only one eating if you don't claim zero," Ryan shot back in an "I wish you would tone." When Ryan pulled up into the Evans' driveway, he was livid and Blake wasn't budging. Blake got out of her truck and went in the house. Ryan realizing that his car was at home, turned off the ignition and followed behind her. When they entered the family room the children were still awake and ran to greet them. Rhoda and Evans had fallen asleep on the kids. Blake and Ryan took them into the twins' room and prepared them for bed. Ryan calmed down realizing how long it had been watching the children prepare for bed. Royce gave Ryan his pajamas, so Ryan could dress him for bed. The look in Royce's eyes always made Ryan love him more than his next breath. The twins got in their beds after a short prayer and Royce clung to his father. Carrying Royce and following Blake to her room, Ryan presented a compromise: "You carry Royce and I carry the twins and Bradley." Blake agreed knowing that Bradley would be 18 this summer and out of their home. "He's living with your mom, right?" Blake asked to make sure. "Yes," Ryan responded in exhaustion. "I'm not laboring to make our new house a home for him to be allowed back inside," Blake said boldly. Feeling like a complete loser, Ryan agreed. The following morning, Ryan drove Blake to work. There was an approved lot for drop offs and pickups that she learned about on her first day. Blake told Ryan about Marvin and how he makes her day. Ryan wasn't concerned about Marvin but Kelvin was on his radar. When Ryan pulled up to the front door, Blake gave him a kiss before gathering her things from the back seat. One of her staff members was across the parking lot in the approved smoking area and saw that she arrived in a Bentley. Blake smirked and told Ryan she was one of the haters. Ryan responded that instead of hating on Blake she should hate how much she resembled a man. The woman's name is Charmaine so Ryan told Blake to call her Mr. Charmaine. Blake laughed and told Ryan she gets off at 3:00. He gave her a salute as she walked away. On his way back home, Ryan asked his connect to run background on Kelvin Franklin. His connect agreed and said he'll have it done within 48 hours. Ryan also decided to put a tracking device on Blake's truck since she thought she was grown. Hours later, Ryan was sitting in a hood spot getting the device added to the truck when Gregory called. The owner rejected his offer but countered with $670k. Ryan agreed upon inspection. Because the current house wasn't yet on the market, he told Gregory he would put 30% down and finance the rest. A few hours later, Gregory called back and told Ryan the offer was accepted and the inspector would be there the following morning. Ryan told Gregory he would meet him there. Knowing the house was solid, Gregory congratulated them and Ryan thanked him. When the truck was ready, Ryan loaded an APP on his phone to track the vehicle. Across town, Blake was finishing up her day. She took in so much information that she couldn't think straight. As her team members dropped off their flash drives, she fought back a laugh when Mr. Charmaine approached her desk. Marvin lagged behind so he could tell her some tea; "Boss lady, rumor has it that you're cheating on your husband with some young dude who drives a Bentley truck." Blake rolled her eyes and replied, "You tell rumor that my husband looks great for his age and the Bentley truck is mine." Marvin's eyes lit up "I knew you was a baddie the first time I seen you... will do."Marvin sauntered off behind the crowd. Blake decided to bring some pictures to work, to sit on her desk. When Blake's schedule ended, she headed for the drop off lot. Though Mr. Charmaine, Irene and Darcy got off at 2:30, they congregated outside the front door. They looked on and gossiped as Blake opened the door to her truck and climbed in the passenger seat and kissed Ryan before they drove away. The women almost fainted when Blake had Ryan stop at Marvin's car for Blake to introduce them. Marvin immediately recognized Ryan. "Oh my gosh I didn't put 2 and 2 together. It's an honor to meet you Pastor," Marvin exclaimed. "I sing on the worship team at Good Shepherd and you preached our Men's Conference." Ryan greeted him in his holy voice and told him he was blessed to meet him. Blake told Marvin she'd see him in the morning and he drove off the lot in joy. Blake was annoyed that her cover was blown. Ryan was glad. He then hoped Marvin would tell everyone so they'd swarm her desk with prayer requests causing her to quit even faster. That evening Ryan took Blake and the children out for dinner and had a slumber party with them in the twins' room. Royce left the party early to sleep with his mother but had a fun time none the less. The following morning on her way to work, Blake was on the phone with Gavin telling him about her new job. His birthday was soon approaching so she asked if her and Bella could stop by to see him. Gavin agreed and told Blake nobody else was allowed to visit him there. Blake agreed and called Bella to arrange a visit the following evening. Bella volunteered to purchase a small ice cream cake and 2 gift cards for their visit. Blake sent Bella $250 for a gift card to Gavin's favorite men's clothing store as a gift for herself, Ryan, and the kids. When Blake arrived at her desk a small box with a bow had been placed in the corner. Hoping Marvin wasn't about to begin "sowing into her anointing," Blake locked away her coat and bags. She decided to answer a few emails before opening the gift. Marvin, who wasn't at his desk when Blake walked through, stopped by to say hello. After a few pleasantries, he assured Blake he didn't and wouldn't reveal to the staff that she was a first lady. He added that he understands the struggle of trying to be yourself under the scrutiny of what others expect you to be. Blake was so thankful and expressed her gratitude to Marvin for being so kind. Blake decided to open the package because it couldn't have been a gift from Marvin. The outward wrapping revealed a blue Tiffany's box. When she opened the box, the small card read: Welcome to the team! Best Wishes, Kelvin. It was a pen. Feeling the gift to be appropriate Blake immediately began to use it. After sending off a few reports, Blake knew Kelvin would soon arrive to get her for Thursdays meeting. When he arrived, Blake was jotting a few important dates into her planner. Before she could thank him for the gift, Kelvin said "I'm so glad you like it." "Yes, I do thank you for being so thoughtful and generous," Blake responded. The two colleagues went to the café to grab their healthy snacks for the long meeting. During the meeting Blake was sure to take notes, she planned on using many of the principles for her mentoring group. She was scheduled to meet the ladies for the first time of the New Year and always loved to challenge their mentalities. After the meeting, Blake went to the cafeteria to grab lunch, surprising Kelvin sat with a friend from another floor. Ryan was overreacting, she thought to herself, Kelvin was just being nice. When her phone rang it was Ryan asking her "Guess who the owners are of 8818 Worthington Circle?" Blake welled up with joy and wanted to walk off the job. Tears fell from her eyes because this meant a fresh new start! Kelvin noticed her wiping away tears and wondered what was going on but decided to ask her privately. Ryan told her the inspector had just finished his inspection and closing was scheduled for Friday, February 14th at 9'oclock am. Blake told Ryan she would request the day off and Ryan told her to hand in her resignation right now. He tempted her with shopping for furniture and décor. Blake had to be strong and stand her ground "does a paycheck come with such fun?" Blake quizzed. Ryan was not about to argue because he had an outdoor kitchen to design. He told Blake to enjoy her workday and ended the call. Blake rushed over to Carla when she saw her standing alone at the beverage console. "Hi Carla, my husband and I just purchased a new home and we're scheduled to close on the 14th of February, may I take the day off?" Blake asked. Carla reminded Blake that she was still in her 90-day training and probationary period and it was frowned upon to miss work. Blake's entire demeanor changed but Carla stood firm. "I tell you what... you choose," Carla said before walking away. Blake immediately called Evans to tell him what happened. Evans told Blake to hold tight. Knowing her daddy is nobody to be played with, she picked up a pumpkin cheese-cake bar and went to her desk. 30 minutes later, Blake received an email from Carla officially announcing to her that her request has been granted. She noticed that Jacob Nance was cc'd on the email. Later that day, Kelvin told Blake that Carla warned all the supervisors to watch their backs with her. She told them about Blake's house and the policy she'd recited because Blake just started working that week. Kelvin went on to say that Carla informed everyone how Blake went over her head and contacted their former Director Jacob Nance and how she only got the job because Blake's father and Nance are old friends. Blake was ready to fight! She was especially pissed because her new home was nobody's business. To add insult to injury she didn't have to work but liked getting out of the house with other adults. Kelvin warned Blake that power plays will turn her into a social leper among leadership. Blake wanted to tell everyone off and walk out like Chris Rock's mother in the hit tv series *Everybody Hates Chris*. When Kelvin walked away Blake called Evans and told him what happened. Evans told Blake to do her job and it would all be okay. She didn't call Ryan because he already told her to quit. By Friday morning, the story had taken on a life of its own behind Blake's back. The gossip mill trickled down from so called leadership to average workers. Marvin told Blake he was willing to tell the story how he acquired it and from who if it were necessary. "Lady B you have God on your side and he don't play about his children," Marvin warned. In that instant Blake smiled. Blake awaited Kelvin's arrival but he didn't show so she called his desk and he didn't answer. Deciding to just study her policy manual, Blake was surprised when Jacob Nance walked up to her desk. He asked Blake to come with him. Blake's staff was looking and whispering having heard that Blake's affair with Nance landed her the job.

When Jacob opened the door, all the senior staffers and

supervisors including Carla were in the room. He asked Blake
to take a seat and she did. Jacob told Blake it had been brought
to his attention that Carla had been accusing he and Blake of
having an affair as the means in which her job was acquired.
Through investigation it was determined when her story
switched from Blake getting the job because of his friendship
with Evans to the current story of an affair. Blake was floored.
She was no stranger to rumors and endured the accusations of
an affair with a former music minister. Much of the staff had
corroborated which version of the story had been told to them.
Kelvin received the story early since he worked closely to her
while others who only met her were given a more salacious
version. Carla had made many enemies over the years and
some were there in opposition to Carla not necessarily in
support of Blake. Because the accusations had been made the
matter of an affair had to be investigated. Blake was asked to
type a statement about how it all happened. Jacob told the
investigators that he received a call from Evans when Blake was
afraid to lose her job for attending the closing purchase of a
home. Blake attested that Carla used the words ..." you choose"
which led her to believe her job was at stake. Carla admitted to
using the statement and that Blake had just met Nance the day
of the interview; remembering that Blake asked him for directions not knowing who he was. Many of the supervisors shook
their heads in disgust. They had jumped on Carla's bandwagon
and hated Blake for no reason. The deputy director insisted
that Carla apologize to Blake in front of everyone since humili-
ating her the same way. Everyone was then dismissed except for
Carla to continue their workday. Hours later, an email was sent
to the staff saying Carla's tenure had ended and the program
wishes her well in her future endeavors. A pin drop could be
heard in the building after the memo went out, everyone knew
she was forced to resign. Marvin sent Blake a direct message
through the internal system which read: "Won't He do it!" Blake

responded: "Indeed He will." Blake felt horrible, she just wanted to peacefully close on her new home. 3 o'clock couldn't come soon enough. Ryan called to ask Blake to dinner but she told him she had plans with Bella. Ryan told her they could celebrate the following night and that he was going to get the children and check into a hotel. Blake thought it was a great idea and agreed to meet them afterwards. Bella and Blake met at Lilly's house to visit Gavin. When he opened the door, he realized how much he missed his family. Gavin had taken the liberty of ordering soul food from around the corner and placed the ice cream cake in the freezer. Blake and Bella caught him up on everything that was going on. They were both floored when Blake told them about Carla and how she spent the major part of her day. Gavin knew Jacob from Evans' stories and shook his head in disbelief. When Lilly came home, she spoke but immediately went into the bedroom and never came out. Bella pretended not to be shocked but Gavin saw it on her face. After dinner they presented him with his gift cards. He was so grateful and thanked them for being so sweet. They sang Happy Birthday and cut the cake. When Bella received a call from Joshua she had to leave. Afterall visiting Gavin was a sting operation. She thanked Gavin for allowing her to come and to Blake for inviting her. The sisters hugged and Gavin walked Bella to her car. When he entered the house, he overheard Blake tell Lilly there was food and cake. Blake always had a way of not shaming people in their mess. Lilly decided to stay out in the living room and asked Blake if she wanted to watch a film. She agreed so Gavin, Blake and Lilly ate cake and watched *The Banker*.An hour later Ryan called Joshua to tell him about the new house. Joshua was excited and congratulated his big brother. When Ryan heard Bella in the background he asked if Blake was at his house. Joshua said no. Ryan told Joshua that Blake said she had plans with Bella. When Joshua asked Bella if she had plans with Blake, Bella said no. Ryan told Joshua he was about to stop by because he had just stopped by the house to grab a few things. The children were playing in their rooms because they hadn't been home in months. Ryan had finally changed the locks and knew Bradley couldn't get inside the house. Ryan ran a location check on Blake's truck and saw it was parked at an unfamiliar address for hours. Ryan texted Blake and asked if her and Bella were enjoying themselves and Blake said they were. Ryan's blood began to boil because he knew she was lying. Ryan gathered the children and told them they were going to visit Uncle Josh. The children cheered because they loved playing with their cousins. Ryan rode around the corner like a bat out of Hades. Ryan knocked on the door and when Joshua answered he asked if the kids could stay for about an hour. Joshua agreed and asked if everything was okay. Ryan told Josh he may have to bail him out tonight. Joshua assumed it was Bradley, Ryan assumed it was Kelvin. When Ryan pulled up to the address, he saw Blake's truck parked out front and his heart began to race. Planning to act a complete fool, he got out of the car. A group of men stood across the street and Ryan pointed to the house asking if they knew who lived there. The men started laughing. The ring-leader of the bunch said "oh yeah, we know who lives there, a player-player from way back," the man said. "Freaks pull up to that house all day long," another said. Ryan's eyes grew wide! How could Blake do this to him? "Yo, dude be banging it out in that bedroom. He has disco lights and freaks stripping on a pole! If we watch from the right angle, we can see the whole show man," another said while the entire group agreed. Ryan repeated the former statement "He bangs it out?" "He bangs it out" they all said in unison. "My wife is in there" Ryan said. "Light-skin with the Bentley?" Ryan shook his head yes. "Yeah she be up in there" the man said. Ryan walked across the street ready to fight. "Holla if you need us" the man shouted. Ryan walked up to the door and banged on it like the police, Gavin jumped up ready to cuss someone out. When the door flew open, both men were shocked. The men watched from across the street ready to have Ryan's back. They were all shocked when Ryan stepped inside and the door was closed behind him. "Maybe old dude is about to cut him in," one of the men said and they all laughed and walked toward the playground to smoke and drink. Ryan was confused. First, he saw Blake talking with Lilly before she ran to the bedroom and now Gavin was crying telling him he was sorry. Ryan looked to Blake for clarity. "Your father and Lilly are together and have been since sometime last year. When my mother told me about it, I stole Lilly's address from the church's database and started coming here to visit him. He swore me to secrecy and with all of our problems I didn't need anymore. Tonight, me and Bella came over to give him a small birthday party but she had to leave because Joshua was looking for her," Blake reported. It was all too much for Ryan to take in. His father was sleeping with one of his parishioners who is younger than Joshua, his mother has been acting like he's been home all along, his wife is secretly visiting his father at his mistress's house and Bradley is on drugs. Ryan was exhausted. "What kind of ungodly mess is this?" he asked his dad. "Son, I'm tired of your mother and her evil ways and just had to do this for me," Gavin sobbed. "You have every right to be happy Dad but this isn't the way! Do you know what your reputation is like in this neighborhood? I thought Blake was in here with her lover from work." Ryan explained. "Kelvin is not my lover," Blake exclaimed. Ryan agreed and told his father the evening has been too much for him. He asked Gavin for his number and told him he'd call in a few days. Gavin wiped his eyes and was angry at himself for falling apart at the sight of his son. Ryan told Blake to meet him at Josh and Bella's. They both got into their cars and drove away. Bella had to admit to Joshua she was part of the birthday sting. Joshua was floored to find out their father was with Lilly

Haskins. Ryan told the three of them what the men on the street told him and everyone was laughing hysterically. The children asked if they could stay and Joshua and Bella agreed. The group made plans to have breakfast in the morning. Blake and Ryan went back to the house to talk and camp out in the loft. Blake finally told Ryan what went down at work and Ryan shared with Blake about his plans for stepping down from ministry and buying into *Taylor Made*. Blake was so excited! Ryan admitted that she deserved her own money but had to admit he couldn't pay her $100k. He told her if she left her job, she could have the profits from 3 of their rental properties which brought in about $3,200.00 per month after property management, insurance, and repair fees. "That's $40k a year to do whatever you want without the tax man eating you to shreds" Ryan added. Blake asked when it would start and Ryan told her March. Blake agreed and asked for some time to learn a few more things before resigning from her position. Ryan reminded her how awful her first week was saying, "too many people believe that opposition is Satan keeping you from some ethereal blessing when most of the time it's God telling you to redirect your attention. We have to stop with this 'pressing through' foolishness because it does more harm than good." Blake agreed and asked Ryan about his shift in theology. Ryan reluctantly shared a few things that Tevin pointed out to him in the scriptures. Blake was floored as she had read those verses hundreds of times. She had to also admit she was taught to assume what they meant but reading them at face value brought an all new revelation. "What church will we attend?" Blake asked. "Ask me that after I take a full year off from attending church at all," Ryan said. "You ain't ready for the freedom of Sundays off, it will change your life," Blake teased. Ryan certainly hoped so. The following Monday, Ryan went to check on Victoria and Bradley. When he got out of the car, Barbara Edwards approached him and asked if they could talk.

Ryan agreed and followed her inside her house. When she offered Ryan a seat her eyes welled up with tears. "I apologize for dropping this on you with no warning but your mother gave me no choice," Barbara began. Ryan sat up in the chair. Tia is in rehab for drug abuse which Bradley introduced her to but her treatment is all the more necessary because she's carrying your grandchild." Barbara said painstakingly. Ryan was blown. "Ms. B when did you tell my mom?" Ryan asked. "During the new year but she fussed at me and put me out of her house calling me a liar," Barbara responded. Ryan apologized for Bradley's collateral damage and told Ms. Edwards that he and Blake would be part of the baby's life upon a paternity test. Ms. Edwards understood and thanked him. Ryan didn't deny Ms. Edwards surety in what was told to her but he knew not to take substance abusers at their word. Meanwhile, Victoria noticed Ryan's car outside and realized he was next door when she saw him leaving Barbara's house. When Ryan knocked on the door, she refused to let him inside. She told Ryan he wasn't welcome in her house if he was willing to believe lies about her grandson. Ryan assured her he just came to check on them. "I spent some time with Dad on Friday" Ryan said through the door. Victoria grew ashamed for lying about them too and walked away. Ryan realized she wasn't going to let him in and drove away. When he got in the car to call Blake, he remembered she was at work. He decided to stop by Brooke's boutique to tell her in person. When Ryan arrived, his cousins Nia, Nya and his Aunt Pat were there. Brooke and Nia often collaborated on fashion stuff so it wasn't odd. He exchanged Happy New Year with everyone and waiting for them to leave to talk to Brooke. Brooke noticed the serious look on Ryan's face and hung the Be Right Back sign on the door and locked it. Brooke invited Ryan into the back-changing area so they could talk. Brook was floored when Ryan told her about Tia Edwards. "I'm too fine to be a grandmother," Brooke said. Ryan was annoyed by her vanity since Bradley's illness was out of control. Ryan sat for a few moments but didn't get the response he was hoping for. He thanked her for her time and left. When Ryan got into his car it was Blake calling him. Relieved to hear her voice, he told her he needed a hug. Knowing something was wrong, Blake inquired about his tone. Ryan told her about Tia and his mother. Blake told him she was so sorry and offered to come by and cook him dinner. He accepted but wished she could come right away. She assigned him the task of shopping for the groceries and picking the children up from school. Immediately he felt comforted and agreed. Blake left work excited for the normalcy awaiting her at home. Though Carla was no longer employed, the residual effects of the rumor mill had lasting effects. Blake found the silver lining at work to be the information she was learning and the opportunity to grow. She hated office gossip and refused to participate. She had a real life with Ryan and her children and knew it was more than most had. She longed for the day when people linked their jealousy to their own decisions. Success is a choice not a circumstance. If nothing else, standing up for herself was a wake-up call to her husband that things needed to change. She decided to listen to Snoh Aalegra's new album, since Lexi wouldn't stop raving about it. The children were playing in the living room when Blake entered the house through the garage. She'd found a charity to donate all the furniture to and planned to let a few of her mentees have the pieces of décor they always admired. After changing into loungewear, Blake came downstairs to cook for the family. Judging by the groceries, Ryan chose meatloaf, mashed potatoes, and spinach for dinner. It had been so long since they were together in their own space so Blake decided to bake some brownies for dessert. Ryan came out of his office and asked Blake if there was room for Gavin. Blake said yes. 30 minutes later, Gavin arrived. They sat down and ate in the formal dining room as a family. Not long after, Joshua rang the doorbell after seeing Gavin's car in the driveway. Blake made him a plate and he sat down to eat while everyone else was having dessert. Bella and the children were at Mumzie and Grandpa Rhodes house. Gavin realized how many people he left by the wayside to seek his freedom from Victoria and planned to visit Mumzie in the morning. He was blessed to still have his mother and should've been more responsible. After dinner, the children had their baths and put on their pajamas because it was a school night. Blake overheard Ryan tell Joshua and Gavin about Tia and her pregnancy and what Victoria did to Barbara Edwards. She decided to watch tv in the loft so they could have some privacy.

Days later, Bradley called Ryan and asked if he and Brooke would meet him for lunch. Ryan told Bradley he would ask Brooke but if she was busy, he would be there regardless. It worked out that everyone was available the same day so they agreed to meet at a popular restaurant. Ryan didn't know what to expect but was prepared for anything. When he arrived, Brooke and Bradley were being seated. When they noticed Ryan, they both stood up to greet him. Brooke was horrified by Bradley's appearance but kept calm. His skin was ashy, his hair texture even changed and he was emaciated. Ryan ask Bradley how he was doing. He told Ryan he was living with his girl-friend Jenna. Ryan asked who Jenna was and Bradley told him it was the girl he met at Victoria's house. Brooke looked at Ryan and he shook his head no. Bradley had a wild imagination if he thought that display of junkie love was a meeting between his father and Jenna. Ryan asked Bradley if he knew he had gotten Tia pregnant and he said yes. "That's why I invited the two of you to lunch to tell you that me and Jenna are having a baby too," Bradley said excitedly. "How are you going to support 2 children with no job?" Ryan asked with his anger rising. "That's the thing, Jenna's rich so we don't need money." Ryan was disgusted! Brooke asked Bradley how Jenna was rich and he told her it was her parents. Ryan mouthed to Brooke silently that Jenna is white. Brooke was too through. Her smoked out son thought Jenna's parents would welcome his addicted black behind into their family. If his appearance wasn't enough, his logic confirmed his illness. Ryan was tired of fighting on every side and looked through the menu in preparation for the waiter's return. Brooke lost her appetite when she saw him and looked around on the dessert menu. She was too sensitive in the stomach not to associate Bradley's appearance with a meal. Ryan ordered a cheesesteak and fries, Brooke ordered apple crisp and Bradley ordered pizza. Ryan asked Bradley if he was feeling better, he said yes. When the food came Ryan ate without talking. Brooke nursed her apple crisp and didn't know what to say. When Ryan finished his meal, he paid the tab, kissed Bradley on the forehead and told him he loved him. Bradley asked Ryan if he was excited to be a grandfather. Ryan looked his son in the eyes and said yes. Bradley smiled the smile Ryan remembered from his childhood and he fought back tears. He told his son a second time that he loved him and Bradley responded with a huge smile, I love you too Dad. Ryan held him in his arms and rocked him and Bradley held his father tight. Ryan kissed him again. "Take care of yourself son, we only get one life." Ryan told him with tears streaming down his face. Bradley shook his head in agreement. "I'm sorry I failed you as a father, please forgive me," Ryan begged. "You didn't fail me Dad, I love you," Bradley responded. Ryan thanked him and held Bradley's face in his hands. Ryan asked Bradley if he'd ever received salvation and Bradley said no. Ryan knew all his children recited prayers with the congregation but needed to make their own choice. He also knew this was an emergency so Ryan led him in prayer. Bradley was surprised that the prayer was different from what he heard week after week in church. Ryan told him that the responsibility to explore his faith was now his own. He held his son again as his heart ached inside his chest. Ryan told Bradley to call him if he needed him and told Brooke goodbye before leaving. When Ryan got in the car, he called Blake. When she answered he could hear Kelvin in the background and couldn't wait for her to resign. His connect had no dirt on him but Ryan had Kelvin's address just in case he had to use it. He told Blake to call him when she was alone and she volunteered to step away. When Ryan told her about Jenna, Blake was floored. "How's he going to raise two kids with no job?" Blake inquired. "He has it all figured out; Jenna is rich" Ryan said mocking the foolery of Bradley's logic. "She's on drugs too, right?" Blake asked. "Absolutely, she was driving a Bentley coupe with dirty bare feet," Ryan countered. Blake told him that Rhoda was dropping the children off to him and she'd be home to make dinner. Blake always knew what he needed. Ryan told her he looked forward to it and how much he loves her. Blake returned the sentiment before ending the call. When Blake pulled into the driveway after work, both her parents' cars and Gavin's car were parked out front. She decided to get the mail before going inside. "Glad you're home first lady," Antoine shouted while entering his house. Blake waved and mouthed a thank you. Before she could walk away another neighbor yelled "we've been praying for you Lady Blake." Blake turned around and mouthed another thank you. When she entered the house, Gavin and Evans were playing cards and her mother was cooking. Ryan was sitting at the island eating the things Rhoda let him taste before dinner was finished. Blake gave Ryan a big hug. He told her his heart hurt and she said hers did too. "Pop is gonna rent this house until he gets on his feet" Ryan told Blake and she said okay. The children were running around playing tag. Blake took a hot shower and put on her footie pajamas. When she got downstairs, Lexi and PJ were there. The sister cousins embraced and had big plans for the new house. Rhoda told everyone to help themselves but made the children's plates. On a Thursday night Rhoda whipped up her famous Cachupa, linguini and clam sauce, fried calamari, baked stuffed shrimp and a 7-up cake. Ryan told everyone about his plans to step down and his 1/3 partnership in *Taylor Made*. Rhoda said she would then pass the intercessory department to Shaye and Treasury to Elder Lawson. Ryan told everyone he and Blake were taking a year off to get things back on track and everyone agreed the respite was long overdue. He went on to tell everyone about the two babies and Brooke's indifference. Everyone listened without adding an opinion. Gavin announced he was divorcing Victoria and added that he was leaving Lilly too. Nobody blinked an eye but were thankful he wasn't staying with Lilly for a myriad of reasons. Blake shared that she was going to leave work by March because her job wasn't feasible for the long-haul. She told the story about Carla and how people believed she had an affair with Jacob Nance to get her job. She went on to add the stigma attached to her even though Carla is no longer there. Rhoda was heated! She was tired of simpletons passing judgement on her precious jewel. Being beautiful and not living hand-to-mouth shouldn't need so much defense. They were lucky she was getting old cause she'd go up to that job and get them all got, one by one. Evans had no idea the job was such a toxic place and planned on going up there to get people got one by one. During dinner, the doorbell rang and it was Grandpa Rhodes and Mumzie. Rhoda shook her head when her father arrived wearing a Fez. Mumzie had blue streaks in her hair and wore blue lipstick to match. Rhodes sat at the island and told everyone they were Black Moors and needed to get in touch with their Asiatic ancestry. "Daddy you're Cape Verdean, so you already knew you were from Africa," Rhoda pointed out. "Girl I'm talking about before the Portuguese came." Rhodes offered. Rhoda gave him a bowl of Cachupa and crusty bread to tap into his heritage. Mumzie cut into the card game and put money on the table. Blake was sad that she had work the following day because her house was lit. She told everyone she had work in the morning but to stay as long as they wanted. "Who told her to get a job?" Grandpa Rhodes asked. "Herself," Ryan answered. Blake and the kids went upstairs to go to bed. Blake slept on the futon in the guest room instead of laying in the loft since everyone was enjoying themselves. She and Ryan still refused to sleep in their bed behind Bradley and usually slept on the sectionals. It wouldn't be much longer before they'd be in the new house. Victoria was sitting in the family room watching television when Gavin entered the house. She had only changed the locks to the front door and forgot he had access from the side. When she saw him, she pretended like he wasn't there. Gavin sat on the ottoman directly in front of her. Gavin thanked her for the decades they've shared together and the family they built. He told her he appreciated everything she'd ever done for him and his family. He praised her for the great men that Ryan and Joshua have become and thanked her for her friendship. Tears began to stream down her face. "You're a good woman Vicky," Gavin said. He took Rhoda's advice to leave her with her dignity. Gavin handed her the divorce petition and Victoria told him she wouldn't contest it. "The house and everything in our account is yours," Gavin said. "I'm broke." Victoria responded. "How?" Gavin asked. "Bradley wiped me out," Victoria admitted. "You gave that boy access to a quarter million dollars?" Gavin asked in a panic. "No, there was only $25k in there," Victoria shot back. "It's a virtual wallet there's $50k in reserve and the remaining $175k is in growth Gavin explained. "You mean to tell me I've been getting food from the local food drive and all along I had $225k?" Victoria snapped. "Don't get mad at me because you don't know how to check on anything," Gavin countered. Victoria felt foolish. Gavin was glad Bradley wasn't smart enough to recognize the other 2 accounts at the atm. Gavin asked if she took the card back from him and she said he claimed he lost it so she reported it stolen. Gavin asked her why she's been covering for his drug abuse. Victoria claimed she didn't know. He asked why she was so disrespectful of Blake. "Gavin you know full well I never liked that girl. Ryan looks better with Brooke," Victoria responded. "Blake is his wife and his first choice so that deserves respect," Gavin added. Victoria didn't agree but her own husband was walking away after almost 50 years; what did she know? Gavin got up from the ottoman and walked into their bedroom to begin packing his things. Victoria asked him where he was planning to live. He told her he was staying at Ryan and Blake's old house because they bought a new one. Victoria was agitated and told Gavin that Blake needed a job. Gavin told Victoria that Blake has a big job with the federal government. Victoria missed it! She longed to see miss thang go to work and help her son. Gavin reminded Victoria that Ryan's life didn't belong to her and if Blake stayed home, she shouldn't have a word to say about it. "You done ruined your relationship with Rhoda, my sister Pat and everyone else. It is not a require-ment to have an opinion about everything that's brought to your attention," Gavin added. "Oh please, they just can't handle the fact that I'm so real," Victoria bragged. "Real lonely" Gavin fired back. "Let me give you some free game Vicky, relation-ships require us to expound upon people's strengths and mini-mize their weaknesses and shortcomings. If you have an opportunity to love again, don't tear the man apart like it's your purpose in life. That goes for women too, be the friend you'd want in return." Gavin explained. Victoria was stung by his words and went back to watch her shows.

5

THE STORM

*R*yan sat in his office at GLC preparing for Jason's transition. The first announcement the congregation received was that Laila and Gerald Canty are the new worship leaders as Jason prepares for pulpit ministry. The congregation was excited and Ryan didn't receive any letters or phone calls. He was amazed by how many sermons he's preached over the last 13 years. He always left a hard copy in his file cabinet. It was also a reminder of his travel schedule. He preached a sermon in most of the states except Arkansas and New Hampshire. He's preached on every continent except Antarctica and his largest live crowd in South Africa had over 200,000 in attendance. He's seen miracles, the mentally dead raised to life and families become whole week by week. He knew many men willing to die in his seat but just as the scripture demonstrates the Good Shepard leaving the 99 to find the 1, he will not lose his family in the pursuit of vain glory. He was already prepared for the over religious crowd whose faulty character, labors to keep people in bondage. The wolves in sheep's clothing who stand in pulpits convincing people that their "demons" must be cast out week after week. They galivant on vacations, drive cars and live in dream homes paid for by their core congregants and "testify" about them as blessings from God. Meanwhile the people live hand to mouth and disregard their dreams in the name of "honor." The Clap back King was ready for Matthew 19:29, Luke 9:62 and the like. He didn't need a 60/85 celebration he wanted a 75th wedding anniversary. Lost in his plans for the future, Ryan didn't hear Elder Lawson when he knocked on the door. "Pastor forgive me for entering but I've been knocking," Lawson said. "I didn't even hear you," spoke Ryan. Lawson informed Ryan that he had a visitor named Ethan Worthington. Ryan didn't recognize the name but told Lawson to let Deacon Vaughn know he was receiving an uninvited guest in the conference room. Vaughn was 1 of 5 men thought to be deacons but were actually armed security. Ryan walked to the conference room since the walls were glass and sat at the head of the table. Deacon Vaughn sat outside on a bench pretending to study the Word. When Lawson returned, he escorted a middle-aged white man into the room "Pastor Ryan this is Dr. Ethan Worthington, Dr. Worthington this is Pastor Ryan Hairston. The two men greeted one another with a smile. When Ryan asked Dr. Worthington what brought him in today, he revealed that he was Jenna's father. Ryan told Dr. Ethan that though he'd never met her, Bradley has mentioned her. Dr. Worthington told Ryan that he hasn't been the best father in pursuit of gaining provision for his family and that all 4 of his children are on drugs. He went on to say that Jenna and his eldest daughter Annie are both pregnant in their addictions and that Jenna names Bradley as the father. Ryan assured Dr. Worthington that he too has dropped the ball in pursuit of what he believed to be the work of God and that Bradley has fallen into substance abuse as well. Ryan told Ethan he and Blake are willing to step up and participate in the baby's life pending a paternity test. Ethan understood as he knew his girls were promiscuous. The two men exchanged stories about their struggles with their drug addicted children and the hopeless-ness that consumes them. Before leaving Ethan asked for prayer telling Ryan that he grew up in a Catholic home and had abandoned his faith in college. Ryan was honored and prayed for Dr. Ethan and his family and their unborn grandchild. Ryan and Ethan exchanged numbers before Deacon Vaughn escorted him to his car.

It was a frigid Valentine's morning when Ryan and Blake sat in Gregory's office to close on their new home. Sitting across from the sellers; the underwriter, loan officer and brokers hashed things out. The Parkers were a pleasant couple who had the home built, were now living in Charlotte, North Carolina. With a large down payment on a 15-year fixed mortgage, the Hairstons' had plenty of wiggle room to build Ryan's outdoor kitchen and furnish the house. They signed on the solid lines and exchanged pleasantries with the Parkers before gathering their belongings. Gregory presented them with a gift as he does all his clients. It was a Hermes Avalon throw blanket in the color Ècru/Gris Foncé. Blake adored it, in her mind the H stood for Hairston. They thanked Gregory for his gift and headed off to lunch. When they arrived at *Farmers Fishers Bakers*, they were escorted to their favorite table. Their waiter, Dante was always happy to see them. The following day, the furniture store was scheduled to bring their new beds. Ryan had just received the call that the delivery window was 8am-12pm. They really wanted to sleep in the house that night and considered buying a few blow-up mattresses. When Dante came back Ryan ordered scrambled eggs with cheese, a NY strip steak, parmesan grits and a cheddar chipotle biscuit from the signa-ture menu. Blake ordered from the same menu but chose eggs over medium, chicken apple sausage, Italian Sunday salad and apple walnut toast. Ryan ordered an Arnold Palmer and Blake chose coffee. After breakfast they stopped by the U-Haul store to buy boxes for their clothes and most of the children's toys.

Blake was keeping her dishes and appliances as they were all well made. She has built up a great collection of *Le Creuset* pots and bakeware and *Crate and Barrel* dishes and serve ware. Since Gavin would be in the house, they were leaving all the large appliances. The previous week they ordered a new smart refrigerator, 2 washers, 2 dryers and a deep freezer. Blake has found it more efficient for the family to be able to wash 2 loads at a time. Their new laundry room was big enough to sit them side by side instead of stacking them like the previous house. Gavin said he needed both sets too because he sometimes works on people's cars or does construction projects for people with Freddie. He liked the idea of cleaning his work clothes in a separate machine. The appliances were scheduled to arrive on Tuesday. Blake enjoyed running errands with her husband in the middle of the day. It reminded her of old times. Her last day of work was scheduled for Friday February 28th and she looked forward to the end. The residual effects of the rumor mill left her exhausted by the end of the day. One of her staff members told some workers in another department that she planned on attacking Blake in the parking lot. She had gotten away with falsifying her research and when Blake caught it, she went on a smear campaign. She called Blake "*Pippi Longstocking*" behind her back saying she acted like an uppity white woman who was a puppet for senior leadership. After 2 additional instances when the worker was caught lying and falsifying her work, she vowed to whoop Blake's behind. If that wasn't enough, an older woman in the research department named Esther, began speaking ill of her too. Blake did nothing to the woman but she didn't like her regardless. Esther told everyone that Blake was "whiter than the Dickens" when Blake wore a pair of ballet flats that revealed the skin tone on her feet. Then there were 2 additional rumors that Blake was dating a female coworker and also having an affair with Kelvin. It was all too much. Blake especially felt bad for Esther, it was rumored that she was in her 70s.

Blake was wise enough to know that nobody wanted to work a full-time job at her age and Esther's anger was misplaced. She simply couldn't afford to retire so Blake became the target of her anger and lack of preparation.

Later that evening Gavin babysat his grandchildren while Blake, Ryan, Joshua, Bella, Jason, Shaye, Lawson, and Ava went on an octuple Valentine's date. The couples decided to go to *Mastro's* as they had much to celebrate. Joshua was just promoted to a tenured professor from adjunct, Bella was promoted within Blake's organization and now responsible for producing the Light Awards™, Lawson and Ryan had their new partnership, Ryan and Blake had a new home and Jason and Shaye would soon step up as the leaders of GLC. The group dined on the seafood tower as well as their favorite entrees. A Live band played music by the bar and all was merry. A few people stopped by the table after recognizing one person or another. It was the perfect ending to a productive day. Ryan and Blake decided to get a room at *The Conrad* as a transition night between the old and the new. After taking a shower together and making love, Ryan surprised Blake with a gift. Surprised to receive one since they just bought a house, she sat up in the bed to open it. Blake pretended to dance and mocked the tune Royce hums when he eats homemade mac n cheese. She opened the beautifully wrapped box to reveal a *Van Cleef and Arpels* yellow gold/malachite vintage Alhambra bracelet with five motifs. Blake's face lit up! Lady Celestine is the queen of *Van Cleef* and Blake always admired her jewelry. Ryan asked if she liked it and Blake told him she loved it so he told her to prove it, with a devilish grin. Blake kissed her husband passionately before disappearing beneath the duvet. The following afternoon, it was all hands-on deck! Some of Blake's mentees were invited over to help themselves to wall prints, vases and other décor items. The Salvation army picked up the children's beds, Blake and Ryan's mattress and foundation, dining furniture and sofa sets. The items had to be placed on the lawn, but they attached a valuation ticket for tax filing purposes. Gavin was keeping Blake and Ryan's bedroom set but ordered a new split foundation and mattress. Gavin ordered wings and pizza and Rhoda created an ice cream bar. In 4 hours flat all of their belongings were boxed and ready to drive to the new house. The new beds arrived for all the bedrooms that morning and Blake had already dressed the beds in clean fresh linens. The new furniture for the common areas of the house wouldn't arrive for the next couple weeks so, they would eat at the patio table in the interim. Blake hung the shower curtains in the children's bathrooms and set up their desks for homework, in their own rooms. As Blake's mentees left, she reminded them of their first meeting of the year the following Saturday and hugged them as they left. The family decided to watch a movie before Blake, Ryan and the children headed home.

An hour into the film there was a knock at the door. When Evans went to answer it, 2 police officers stood outside. "Good evening Sir, we're looking for Mr. Ryan Hairston," said one officer. Evans called for Ryan whose stomach dropped to his feet when he saw the flashing red and Blue lights. "Are you Ryan Hairston?" The officer asked. Ryan said he was. "I'm terribly sorry sir but there's been an accident and your son Bradley has passed..." Ryan heard nothing else as his legs buckled beneath him. Ryan let out a painful sound impossible to describe. As Blake rushed around the corner, she saw her husband on his knees in anguish. "Daddy what's wrong?" she asked Evans who told her Bradley had passed away. Blake's mind struggled to make sense of his words and her body began to tingle. She struggled to stand but couldn't feel her legs. Joining Ryan on the floor, all she could do is rock back and forth in a daze. The police told Evans that someone needed to identify the body and Evans told them they would do so in the morning. Everyone rushed to the door and were shocked to hear the news. The children were confused by the commotion and began to cry. Rhoda held all three of them and held them tightly. Gavin leaned up against the wall as tears streamed down his face. Joshua and Bella cried silently and held on to their children. It was a long night! Once able to get off the floor, Ryan called Brooke to deliver the news. He didn't ask her how she felt or offer any comfort because he didn't care. She hasn't seemed concerned but only disgusted by their son and Ryan considered her cancelled. He also called Devin, his best friend and the children's godfather. Blake called Lexi who drove all the way from Virginia to be by her side while Paris stayed with the kids. Paris called Parrish and Pat. Pat called Courtney and Nia. Gavin sent Joshua and Bella to tell Victoria because he knew she would take it hard. Gavin called his mother Mumzie and Rhoda's father Rhodes. Rhoda called her sister Vivian who told her husband Alex. Evans called his sons who lived out of state and were Blake's brothers. Ryan called Tevin who took it hard because he never saw it coming. He was rooting for Ryan to recover all and his own pain still ached and was raw. Tevin told Ryan he would be there in a couple days. The family stayed all night. Ryan, Royce and Blake laid on the futon in the guestroom because Gavin wanted to keep it. The twins slept in their sleeping bags and Rhoda and Lexi laid beside them. Lexi had prototypes for her new bedding collection in her truck and laid blankets and a few pillows out so everyone could have some comfort. Gavin laid on the chaise from the patio, Evans sat in the recliner and Freddie laid on an air mattress. Nobody could sleep except the children and the family knew they had a long road ahead. The following morning as he prepared to identify Bradley's body, Ryan received a call from Ethan Worthington. He offered Ryan his condolences and informed Ryan that Jenna was in a coma. Ryan offered his sorrow for her condition before asking Ethan if he knew what exactly happened. Ryan heard nothing the police told him the night prior after hearing that Bradley was gone. Ethan told Ryan that according to Annie, they were all at his residence getting high. Someone noticed that Bradley had over dosed and everyone panicked. In an attempt to carry him to the shower, the group dropped him causing him to hit his head. When they noticed him bleeding, they decided to drive him to a nearby hospital. Bradley's two friends Jerry and Cameron, put him in the back seat of Jenna's SUV, Jenna drove, Cameron was in the passenger seat and Jerry rode in the back with Bradley. Annie, her best friend Allie and Jenna's best friends Heather and Abby, followed closely behind. According to Annie, the truck began swerving halfway to the hospital as if some sort of commotion was going on inside the car. Soon after, according to Annie the car veered over into oncoming traffic and collided head on with a tow truck, which pushed the truck back over into the lane of an oncoming vehicle before driving into a light pole. None of them had on a seatbelt. Jenna was ejected through the windshield, Cameron was found hanging out of the broken passenger side window, Bradley was catapulted to the front of the truck and Jerry was still in the back seat. Tears streamed down Ryan's face as he listened to Annie's account as told by Ethan. Ethan mentioned that though he didn't know the condition of the other two young men, he did know that Jerry's father was also a pastor. Ryan asked Ethan what Jerry's last name is and Ethan said he would ask Annie and text it to him when he found out. Ryan agreed and told Ethan to keep in touch. Ethan told Ryan he was in his thoughts and prayers. Ryan felt faint standing over his first-born child, lifeless on a cold metal slab. Accompanied by his father who stood behind him to hold him up, Ryan's heart was shattered into pieces. Gavin who never imagined burying a child, was now faced with burying a grandchild. The two men stood in silence, in pain and in regret. The medical examiner told Ryan he would have the results on Bradley's autopsy within 24 hours. Ryan told the examiner that

Bradley's DNA needs to be harvested for two future paternity tests. The examiner gave Ryan a form to fill out so his blood can be drawn and properly maintained until the tests were complete. Ryan also had to pay for its proper storage. Ryan was thankful that he made Blake stay home. Why should she have to endure this kind of pain when Brooke refused to do so. "I was there when he was born and you weren't so, we're even," said Brooke when Ryan asked if she'd go with him. Brooke's attitude continued to chip away at her beauty in Ryan's eyes. When other men saw Brooke, they always complimented him on having a "bad" baby momma. Though Blake didn't garner the same type of response, she was wife material and a true lady. Blake was a big hit with the academic, professional, and wealthy crowds. Brooke was hot in the streets. Disturbing Ryan from his thoughts, Gavin told him it was time to go. Ryan began to breath heavy and broke down in tears. Gavin held him as the coroner placed a white sheet over Bradley's head and pushed the slab back into the refrigerated drawer. Gavin wept, holding his first born as he mourned his, was a tough pill to swallow. Ryan was so weak and broken that Gavin had to walk him to the back seat of his truck so he could lay down. Gavin strapped him into the seat belt like he did when Ryan was a little boy. Fighting back his own tears, Gavin climbed into the front seat of his truck. "Daddy don't take me home, just drive," Ryan sobbed. "North or South?" Gavin asked. Ryan said north so after texting Blake, Gavin drove all the way to New Jersey and back. Back at the old house, food began to arrive from family and friends. Blake had spoken to Shaye early that morning and said it was okay to tell the congregation. Blake also left a message on the interim director's voicemail at work, who returned her call offering his condolences and telling Blake it was okay to resign early. She had just received her paycheck the day before and was shocked to have earned $2656.23. She still had another paycheck coming on the 28th. After all her troubles, Blake was definitely treating herself to something nice. She was glad that she didn't go to the morgue and preferred to be home with the children. Rhoda bathed the kids and dressed them in comfortable clothes. She knew they fully couldn't comprehend what was happening but they were all told that Bradley was gone. Not knowing any better, Royce clapped saying "yaaay" and Rhoda had a feeling Ryan heard him doing so. When the doorbell rang, assuming it was more food, Blake was overwhelmed to find Devin, Zoe and their godson DJ, aka Sire, at the door. Devin's eyes were welled with tears and all they could do was cry together. By evening: Pat, Parrish, Courtney, Texan, Paris, PJ, Pierre, Lexi, Vivian and Alex, Mumzie and Grandpa Rhodes were at the house. Evans and Freddie rented seating and tables so everyone could be more comfortable. The whole moment was sobering. Parrish said he knew it wasn't an identical situation but he remembered the horror the family endured years prior when Nya was kidnapped. Blake remembered that time more than anyone because she had just returned to Nia's care after spending years in Blake's custody. When Blake asked where Nia and Nya were, Pat reluctantly said they were with Brooke. In an awkward moment, everyone grew silent knowing Nia and Brooke being close came after her fall out with Blake. Though they made up, it was better for them to be cousins than friends. Blake remembered the day Ryan told Nia off about her treatment of his wife and things were never the same. Lexi also kept a bit of distance from her sister-in-law because Blake was her blood. It was the first time Devin was in such close proximity to the Lovehalls' since divorcing Nia. He was glad she was with Brooke because he could go the rest of his life without seeing her face, though circumstances such as this made it impossible. It was 7pm by the time Gavin and Ryan returned from their excursion. Blake informed everyone that Ryan had to identify Bradley's body and wanted some time alone with Gavin. When Ryan entered the house, he was surprised that the family was there waiting for him. When he saw Devin, they fell into each other's arms and cried together. Devin was there when Ryan met Brooke in undergrad. The best friends had weathered each other's storms for over 20 years and this time was no different. Blake convinced Ryan to eat something and the two of them, Devin and Zoe ate at a card table in the formal dining room. Gavin told his sister Pat and the rest of the family that he and Victoria were getting a divorce. He also told them that he was staying in the house since Ryan and Blake bought a new one. Everyone wondered where the furniture was but felt it inappropriate to ask. "They were on their way to stay in the new house after a day of packing up, when the police came," Gavin explained. Everyone was saddened. Mumzie couldn't believe she outlived a great grandchild! Life can be so cruel. Across town, Joshua, Bella, and the children were still with Victoria. She spent the entire night crying. While Joshua was bringing groceries in that morning, he informed Barbara Edwards that Bradley had passed away. Barbara was shocked and told Joshua to offer her condolences to Ryan and Blake. She told Joshua it was family day at the treatment center and would ask Tia's sponsors if it was okay to alert her to Bradley's passing. Joshua said he would relay the message before entering the house. Later that day, Barbara knocked on Victoria's door. Deciding to demonstrate her Christianity, her and a few neighbors brought over some food, flowers, and desserts. Remembering what Gavin said, Victoria was kind and pleasant. Encouraging Joshua and Bella to get some rest, Barbara assured them she would keep Victoria company. Convicted by Barbara's kindness, Victoria apologized for her actions. Barbara accepted and made her a plate. After telling his mother he'll check on her later that day, Joshua, Bella and the children, headed home. While driving home, Joshua saw all the cars at Blake and Ryan's so he decided to check on them before heading home. When he entered the house, the entire family was there to greet them. Everyone hugged and exchanged sentiments of love. When Gavin inquired about Victoria, Joshua told his father that Barbara Edwards and a few neighbors came over to sit with her. Gavin was glad the old crow decided to be nice. Asking the Lord to forgive his thoughts, he was glad she took his advice. Before the night was over, Jason and Shaye stopped by to bring some food and offer their condolences. Ryan told Jason if the coroner was finished by Wednesday, the funeral would be Saturday. Jason told Ryan that Lady Celestine and Bishop sent their condolences and Lady offered to make the programs. Ryan told Jason to thank her and accepted the help. Blake usually did the programs for families but she and Ryan agreed to accept all the help that was offered. Ryan introduced Jason and Shaye to the Braxton's. Devin told Jason he was a huge fan and named a few of his favorite songs. "I was there at your show in Chicago when you had the *Ultra Bed* on stage," Devin added. Everyone laughed. Jason sometimes thought of his days as a superstar and understood the hold drugs had on Bradley. He couldn't imagine being addicted that young. Surely it was God who spared him. Late that evening, The Hairstons and the Braxtons headed to the new house to get some sleep. Parrish, Pat, Courtney, and Texan headed back to Hampton. Vivian, Alex, Lexi, Paris, PJ and Pierre headed back to Arlington, Mumzie and Grandpa Rhodes went home just miles away, Joshua, Bella and the children went home around the corner and Rhoda and Evans drove home as well. Freddie stayed in the old house with Gavin and everyone attempted to get some rest. On their way back to Hampton, Pat told Parrish that she was glad Gavin decided to be happy. She knew it wasn't right but Victoria had really changed over the years. Courtney was so grateful that she and Texan's children were healthy and whole. Tomorrow wasn't promised and she told her parents they needed to keep up with the family like they used to. The Lovehalls' agreed. Blake told

Ryan that Nia and Nya were with Brooke. Ryan looked in the rearview mirror and caught eyes with Devin who smiled overtly. "They deserve each other," said Devin as everyone remained silent. Riding in the opposite direction, Lexi told Paris how much she appreciated him for always being a present father. He thanked her for being a great mom. "Who knew it would get this bad?" asked Paris. "I knew the night he spit on Blake changed the family dynamic forever but never did I see this as the outcome," Paris added. Lexi shook her head as tears streamed down her face. Across town Brooke, Nia and some of their friends played boardgames and uno. Many of them brought food, desserts, liquor, and flowers for Brooke's comfort. The kids played among themselves and Brooke's boyfriend "Black" had his friends over to play Spades. Black never met Bradley though he dated Brooke for the past 9 months. Her ex-husband, Arrington Thompson was married to Brooke for 7 years before their divorce just 18 months ago. Arrington is a master chef and restauranteur who Brooke met through Nia's ex-husband Garrett. Since then, Brooke chose to catch flights and not feelings. Nia found it strange that Brooke never cried. She knew everyone grieved differently and chose not to pass judgment. She wondered what her family was doing at Blake and Ryan's. She knew Devin would be in town at some point and wished she could turn back time.

Rhoda was exhausted. She told Evans she wanted to be on a beach once everything was over. Grateful for the opportunity to always be there for her children and grandchildren, Rhoda had been stretched to the end of her sanity. She planned to call Kenneth the following day and tell him about Bradley's passing. She knew Blake would feel good seeing him if he was able to come.The next morning, Ryan looked at his phone for the first time in 24 hours. He was shocked to see the text from Ethan that read: Jerome Headley Jr. Jerome senior was the pastor of Shine your Light ministries in Rosaryville that partners with GLC annually for community outreach. Ryan immediately called. When Jerome answered the phone, Ryan greeted him and told him he just learned that their sons were in an accident together. When Jerome asked how Ryan's son was, Ryan told him that Bradley was deceased. Jerome offered Ryan his family's condolences and said Jerry was paralyzed. The two fathers compared notes and realized the two boys were close. Ryan told Jerome that Jenna was in a coma supposedly carrying Bradley's child. Jerome stated that Jenna told Jerry the baby was his. Ryan secretly hoping it was Jerry's child said they would know for sure upon paternity. Jerome offered his condolences again and told Ryan he would tell Jerry about Bradley's passing. He also told Ryan that Cameron was the 4th person in the car and he was in a coma as well. "His parent's attend my church. His father is state representative Joseph Brooks and his mother is anchorwoman Addie Brooks," said Jerome. Ryan told him to relay his sympathy to their family and knew who both of them were but never met them.

Later in the day, Dr. Worthington called Ryan to tell him he called in a favor. The media would update the story not to include the children's drug use. "we all have enough to deal with without our family names being smeared in the media," Ethan spoke. Ryan thanked him for doing so and told him they'd speak soon. By late afternoon, the medical examiner called Ryan and concluded that Bradley was deceased before the accident and all of the injuries sustained by the car crash were postmortem. He told Ryan the cause of death was cardiac arrest due to cocaine overdose. He added that though crystal meth was found in his system in small amounts it was the cocaine that killed him. He added that Bradley had a heart defect that must've gone undetected, which compromised his health. Ryan thanked him and told him the undertaker would come for Bradley's body soon. Ryan called his congregant William Bivins and told him Bradley's body was ready for transport. Bivins Funeral Home had served Ryan's congregation from the start and Ryan trusted the family to prepare his son's final arrangements. Willie offered his condolences to Ryan on behalf of the family and added "Pastor, I spoke to Beverly about this beforehand and we'd like to sow our services and Bradley's coffin as a gift for all you and Lady Blake have done for us." Ryan fought back tears and thanked them for their generosity. "Any package you want Pastor, we have your back," William added. Ryan ended the call and took a deep breath. He called Brooke and asked her if Bradley had a heart defect. She told him he was born with some heart issues but she assumed he outgrew them. Instead of arguing with her, Ryan told her his cause of death was cardiac arrest due to cocaine intoxication but the heart defect made him less likely to survive. She thanked him for calling and asked when the funeral was so she could close the boutique annoyed by her cavalier demeaner, Ryan told her Saturday. He abruptly hung up because he felt a cuss out creeping up his spine. When Ryan told Blake all that he learned during the calls, she wept in sadness. She too hoped that Jenna's baby didn't belong to Bradley because they were almost certain that Tia's baby did. The day was filled with calls, arrangements, and questions. Joshua brought food to the new house that had just arrived at the old house. Gavin couldn't fit any more food into the refrigerator. An email went out to the congregation telling them to refrain from sending food to the house because Pastor and First Lady had moved. Only a couple dozen congregants knew their home address but were also sending food on behalf of those who didn't know it. When Zoe opened the pans to make everyone's plates there was mac n cheese from Elder Lawson's grandmother Hattie, corned beef and cabbage from Blake's fellow New Englander sister Yara, fried fish from Deacon Shelton, green beans and collards from sister Tootie, lasagna from sister Jan, smoked ribs from brother Riley, chocolate cake from Mother Watts, carrot cake from

Brother Dixon and banana pudding from sister Kelly which Gavin tried to keep. The children ate lasagna and everyone else tasted everything. Rhoda called after hearing from Evans who heard from Gavin that the banana pudding was at the house. Everyone fought over Kelly's banana pudding and many a race and arm wrestle took place over the last bowl. Kelly was old school and made it from scratch. Legend has it that her banana pudding caused brother Joe to propose.

By Thursday morning everything was finalized. Prophet Tevin came in town without the children so Ryan insisted that he stay at the house. The family took the time to rest because they knew Saturday would be an extremely long day. Blake insisted that the women wear creams and winter whites instead of black. Pastor Elisha would eulogize Bradley and Lady Nora would keep the flow of service. Ryan and Blake, Tevin, Devin, Apostle Sands, Pastor Josiah and Lady Joelle were schedule to speak. Jason Kemp and Lady Celestine were scheduled to sing. Rhoda and Shaye were scheduled to pray and Bradley's 8th grade teacher Miss Lewis, would read the scriptures. GLC was packed to the gills. The outpour of love for the family was tangible giving Ryan a strength he didn't know he possessed. Faces he and Blake hadn't seen in years offered words of comfort in peace during the procession. As the family took their seats on the front row, Bishop Kemp and Lady Celestine, Pastor Elisha and Lady Nora and Apostle Sands and Lady Eleanor sat on the pulpit. Pastor Elisha and Lady Nora stood to greet the crowd on behalf of the family. Introducing themselves as Ryan and Blake's spiritual parents in the faith, they each testified of Ryan and Blake's love for God and His people. Lady Nora opened in prayer and told all in attendance that the viewing was set to begin, starting with those in the overflow and standing in the hallway citing "as it is in the kingdom of God, the last shall be first," said Lady Nora. The worship team began to play as those not seated in the sanctuary and those with no seat at all, came to view the body and offer condolences to the family. As the mourners came down the aisle, some of Ryan and Blake's friends from high school were in the crowd. Amazed that so many of them kept up with the couple, brought them great comfort. Community partners and old parishioners came to offer their respects. Many who did the couple dirty came to apologize for the things they had said or done to harm the couple. Blake was blown away to see Marvin and thanked him for coming. She was just as stunned to see Kelvin and introduced him to Ryan. She knew for sure her cover was blown when the news broke the story. As the crowd began to proceed from the back of the sanctuary Ian and Jasmine came to show their respects with their brood. Cashmere, Chiffon and Silk were gorgeous children as was Cashmere's daughter. Joelle saw Jasmine aka Apple from the 3rd row and blew her a kiss. Dr. Worthington and his wife Karen paid their respects, Pastor Jerome, and his wife Lady Shamika were also in attendance and Cameron's father representative Brooks who gave Ryan his card. Blake's classmates from Towson and coworkers from the Library of Congress were also in attendance. Ryan and Blake were so moved to see Deaconess Ava's father Deitrick and step-mother Bernie. Blake was also surprised to see her biological father Kenneth and knew Rhoda must've called him. He told Ryan and Blake that he came to show his face but had to leave during the service to fly to California on business. Ryan thanked him for stopping in and Kenneth handed Blake a wad of cash before kissing her on her forehead and telling her he loves her. Ryan turned to Blake and said your father coming just to show you he cares is the bomb. Blake agreed and felt her father's encompassing love for the first time since being a child. Mentees from times past and present showed up in numbers for the couple. Blake cried when she looked up to see JT and Ardena and held her good friend so tight. Their neighbors from the old house also came in record numbers. Ryan's barber,

Blake's nail tech, masseuse and hair stylist came too. The manager of the grocery store and Rayne's ballet teacher came as well. As the lines tapered down. Lady Nora called the viewing to a close for the beginning of service. Ryan, Blake, and the children stood before the casket to say their final goodbyes. The twins walked away and went to sit with Rhoda at the end of the row. Royce put his head on Ryan's shoulder and rubbed his back. His tiny hands brought Ryan to tears. Blake's arm was firmly around Ryan's waist as she remembered the great times she and Bradley shared. Ryan told Blake to take Royce and sit down. Realizing Ryan had no intention of sitting down anytime soon, Brother Bivens sat down and planned to close the lid later. Lady Nora accepted the obvious and went along with the service. Josiah mounted the platform and offered his condolences to the family before taking a quick text. He spoke on the importance of the Village. Offering that we are our brother's keeper, he charged the village to stop looking out for just themselves. "We all have a collective responsibility to look out for one another. In our pursuit of the newest and the best, we've lost sight of our love and compassion," Josiah ended. He offered the antidote to the listening crowd: live, act and walk in love. The congregation said Amen! Victoria broke down in tears because she knew she enabled Bradley to his detriment. Josiah stopped by the casket to hug Ryan who was holding Bradley's hand and rocking. Someone brought him a chair so he could sit down. Tevin interceded for Ryan the entire time as did Rhoda. Joelle mounted the platform and reiterated the love and appreciation she and Josiah had for the Hairstons'. Joelle didn't take a text but spoke from her heart. Citing that her subject matter is *A Mother's Love*. Using examples from the past and present, Joelle laid out an immaculate depiction of the unrelenting and unconditional love of a mother. Joelle used the story of Rizpah in the old testament who stayed with the decaying bodies of her sons, day and night for months to keep scavengers away until King David agreed to bury their bones. She spoke of women whose love and strength undergirded nations. Joelle illustrated Blake's love and dedication to her children which is of great value and sacrifice. Of her mothering the church and its members into health and wholeness. Lady Celestine stood up and shouted, "Go on and preach then!" Feeling the pull of the crowd, Joelle spoke of the work Blake did behind the scenes to hold the church together for which Lady Celestine shouted again "honey tell the truth." Joelle told the congregation that other speakers may be sent to speak about Bradley but God sent her to assure Blake that her labor of love has not gone unseen and The Father said: "Well done!" Blake broke down in tears as Lexi comforted her. Ryan stood to clap and everyone stood to give Blake a standing ovation. Joelle walked up to Blake and the one-time best friends held each other and cried. During the time of celebration Miss Lewis came to the mic. When the crowd settled down, she told a story about Bradley and Blake winning the 8th grade mother and son dance competition. Everyone laughed when Ms. Lewis talked about Blake dressing up like a rapper because Bradley picked out her costume. Blake shook her head in agreement. Adding to what Joelle said, Miss Lewis told the congregation that Blake never missed a thing. "Bake sales, sporting games, science fairs and talent shows, Mrs. Hairston was there. Miss Lewis did the scripture reading for which she had been assigned and stepped down from the platform. Jason stood up to sing as Ryan requested: *Reckless Love* written by Caleb Culver, Cory Asbury and Ran Jackson. There wasn't a dry eye in the house from the first word. Jason has a way of singing that nobody on the planet possessed. When he got to the chorus Ryan stood with his hands raised *"Oh the overwhelming, never-ending reckless love of God, oh it chases me down, fights till I'm found leaves the 99. I couldn't earn it; I don't deserve it..."* The congregation sang in unison. By the end people were shouting and Lady C was waving her rhinestone studded lace hankie. "I taught him that," she shouted. Jason hugged Ryan who still was at the casket and Blake before crossing the aisle to hug Brooke before sitting down. Devin mounted the platform to speak a few words. Nia who was sitting with Brooke and Victoria couldn't help but stare. She hasn't been in a long-term relationship since the divorce from her ex-husband Garret and Devin was her first love. Devin offered his condolences to Ryan, Blake, and Brooke. Telling the congregation, the great times he, Ryan and Brooke had in college. Devin spoke about how proud he was to have Bradley as one of his godchildren. Using the screens on the sides of the pulpit, he showed pictures of a fishing trip that he, Ryan, and Bradley went on. He also showed the aftermath of Bradley panicking because he caught an eel, causing all three of them to fall into the water. "The brat forgot how to swim and said he was drowning until Ryan told him to stand up," Devin laughed. Everyone was laughing hysterically. "One of the reasons I'm mad that he's gone is because I was waiting for him to get his first job to replace my Gucci shoes," Devin joked. "I'm taking the watch off his wrist," Devin added as everyone laughed themselves to tears. When Devin hugged Brooke, Nia could smell his cologne and caught butterflies in her stomach. Devin acted like he didn't see her and walked away. When he hugged Ryan, he acted like he was reaching for Bradley's wrist. In all the hysterics, Tevin mounted the platform. In his crowd catching manner, accusing Joelle of stealing his message and feminizing it, he spoke on the role of a father. Tevin used his testimony of being too busy in ministry to build his own home. Citing that he was an absent father in the name of The Father. Tevin illustrated the contrast between himself and Blake saying, "she missed nothing, I missed everything." Saying he had Ryan's permission to say that he too was falling into the same trap. Tevin shared about Gabby's passing and how fast she slipped away. Telling every listener that it was just weeks prior that Ryan and Blake sat beside him on his front row. He reminded every father and husband to stand in their true assignments. "I know I'm messing with many people's theology but ministry can wait. The poor and hurting will always be among us but our children will never get younger and our wives won't wait forever." Tevin told the congregation it was time to grow up and stop sucking the life out of their leaders. All the senior leaders in the room shouted Amen. Tevin publicly told Ryan to hold his family tight and never allow the church to kill him since Jesus already died. Tevin greeted Brooke and Victoria but gave Ryan a bear hug and spun Blake around before taking his seat. Lady Celestine mounted the platform dressed to kill. Wearing a hi-low cream silk bubble dress and 5-inch single soled rhinestone pumps. She and Blake had a saying that *real ladies keep their shoes on the entire time; You gotta pay the cost if you want to floss!* "When I thought about which song to minister today, I caught a vision of Bradley standing before the throne in all white and knew which song to sing. Ryan, Blake and Brooke I don't claim to know exactly what you're going through but I know where Bradley is!" said Lady C. The music began and she ministered the Bart Millard written classic, *I Can Only Imagine* as performed by Tamela Mann. Tevin especially broke down picturing Gabby the exact way. Ryan stood to watch her minister: *To be surrounded by your glory, what will my heart feel? Will I dance for you Jesus? Or in awe of you be still? Will I stand in your presence? To my knees will I fall? Will I sing Hallelujah? Will I be able to speak at all? I can only imagine...I can only imagine.* Blake stood as everyone sang the song's war cry: "Oh-oh-oh-oh, Oh-oh-oh-oh, Oh-oh-oh-oh, Oh-oh-oh-oh, Oh-oh-oh-oh-oh-oh-oh, Oh-oh-oh-oh." Lady Celestine adlibbed "*I see Bradley with the King, I see Bradley with the King, Ryan your prince isn't here he's standing before the King.*" Her words brought Ryan such comfort that he rejoined Blake and brother Bivins removed Bradley's jewelry, lowered the body, and closed the casket. He handed the jewelry to Ryan who gave it to Blake to put inside her purse. Shaye mounted the platform to pray for the family and tore the roof off the place! Rhoda knew she trained her well and felt good knowing the intercessory team was in great hands. The 7-minute prayer soothed the aching hearts of the family and lifted the spirits of all in attendance. Hugging Shaye as they approached the pulpit Ryan and Blake mounted the steps holding hands. Ryan reached for Brooke but she snatched back her hand. Wearing a cream peplum suit and her signature nude pumps and nude lipstick Blake was the epitome of class. Lady Celestine shouted, "I see you mini me, that's how you feel?" which made Blake turn to blow her kisses. Ryan thanked everyone for coming. "We never in a million years, thought we'd be standing here saying goodbye to our son, I'd like to thank Brooke for blessing me with my life's greatest lesson," spoke Ryan. Everyone clapped for Brooke and she stood up to wave to the crowd. Ryan squeezed Blake's hand which was code for *"This heifer wants glory without the hard work, she needs to sit down."* Blake looked at Ryan and giggled. Ryan told everyone to hold their families tight and to make sure everyone they love, knows it. Blake expressed her appreciation for the outpour of love and comfort. Ryan introduced Grandad and Apostle Sands walked over to preach the eulogy. Apostle taught on the importance of family as so many before him spoke. He told everyone that family was worth fighting for. He highlighted some of Bradley's accomplishments in playing the keyboard and in sports. He told a story about Bradley taking all the candy from his foyer but leaving one piece behind as if he'd done alms. It was short but sweet. Lady Nora read some of the resolutions before Rhoda closed out in prayer for those in attendance. After Rhoda wrecked the place with a charge to do better, Jason and his fabulous mother Lady C came together to sing the closing song for the recessional. To leave on a high note and seal the prayer that Rhoda prayed they chose the A'Leithia Sweeting penned worship tune Let Praises Rise as sang by Miranda Curtis and Micah Blalock. Apostle Sands accompanied by Lady Eleanor followed the casket as he recited scriptures and prayed walking down the center aisle with the pulpit guests following him. Lady Celestine walking with Bishop Kemp held her microphone, Ryan and Blake followed behind them. Brooke was behind them. After Apostle Sands shut off his microphone a heavenly medley flowed out of Lady C and Jason as their voices meshed perfectly *"All I want is for you, for you to be glorified, for you to be lifted high, all I want is for you, for you to be glorified, for you to be lifted high"* The spirit was high and Lady C stopped to *sing her face off facing Jason still on the pulpit with the band "Fill my heart till all they see is you Lord glory your name."* The procession stopped as her and Jason sang in a heart stomping rendition back and forth vocally sparring. People danced in the aisle and the pall bearers swayed back and forth. Ryan felt 100 pounds lighter though he knew there would be some painful days ahead.After going to the cemetery, Blake and Ryan were exhausted. They joined the private dinner the church prepared for them with close friends and family in lieu of a repass. Kelly made 5 banana puddings to settle all grievances and disputes. After dinner, Rhoda and Evans took the children with them so Blake and Ryan could rest. When Sire asked if he could come, they took him too. Victoria walked up to Blake to tell her how beautiful she looked and to give her a hug. Blake received the gesture and returned the love. Victoria told Blake they should have lunch soon and she agreed. Blake always left room in her heart for people to grow but especially wanted to be cordial with the mother of her king. By the time Ryan, Blake, Devin, Zoe, and Tevin made it back to the house it was late in the evening. Tevin told Blake he needed some time but he wanted to meet the red head she was talking to. Blake told him that was her hair stylist Anastasia. "Next year around this time," Tevin said. Blake agreed. The weeks following Bradley's burial flew by in record numbers. Ryan went to the church to move out of his office for good as Jason's installation was just a couple weeks away. Ryan thought about all the people he and Blake served and knew they did their due diligence. Their true ministries as mentors and counselors would be part of who they are forever. When cleaning out one of his cabinets, Ryan found Blake's old schedule when she was pregnant with Royce. His eyes welled up with tears as he recounted the stress he ignored back then:

- Drive Bradley and the twins to/from school M-F
- Pick up Davina from school M, T, R, F
- Take Bradley to soccer practice M, W, F
- Take Rayne to ballet practice T, W, R
- Take Ryan Jr. to swimming lessons M, R
- Make breakfast, lunch, and dinner (pack lunches if kids don't want school lunch)
- Clean Bathrooms M, W, F
- Do Laundry T, R, Sat
- Clean bedrooms W, Sat
- Go grocery shopping T, Sat
- Drop off dry cleaning, W
- Pick up dry cleaning, F
- Light Awards conference call M @9pm
- Women's ministry conference call W@8pm
- Facilitate morning prayer call T @6am
- Women's bible study facilitator T (next 8 weeks)
- Meet with mentees 2nd Sat and 4th Sunday
- Speak at prayer breakfast on the 17th
- Teach at women's conference on the 22nd
- Dry run of awards gala on the 30th

The tattered page reminded Ryan that he's taken his wife for granted more times than he remembered. He also realized in place of all the delegated responsibilities to others, Blake always seemed to acquire new ones. Women are so amazing he thought, especially his. Among the files he read letters from members expressing their appreciation, which he put in a pile to be kept as keepsakes. He read through letters from angry members who left as those he wasn't called to serve. One thing he has learned in his years of pastoring is that some members who are attracted to your ministry, aren't meant to be there. It wasn't that he was a bad leader or that they were bad people but they were just misplaced. Ryan wasn't seduced by the faithfulness of his flock but with being itinerant. The seduction of traveling the world and being treated like a Rockstar for preaching is intoxicating. It's why Jason held such a special place in his heart. Jason has already overcome the roar of crowds and the idolization that comes with fame. Ryan experienced church fame which is much more insidious. The number of people able to be harmed spiritually because of your personal decisions has greater implications. Celebrities are allowed to be amoral but preachers are expected to possess self-control. He knew Jason could cast a wider net in the name of Truth. The church is such a loyal institution that its members are more content in the comfort of falsehood than to accept the uncomfortable truths. Their own bible reads that *Faith without works is dead*, yet they will sit idly by "waiting on the Lord." His prayer for Jason is that he could elevate the thinking of the congregation. Too many saints leave their intellect at home in favor of emotion which they mislabel as the Spirit. It was time for the naked truth to get his garments back from the well-dressed lie; as told by Jean-Léon Gérôme, in 1896. By the late afternoon Ryan packed up all his family's belongings and moved out of the church. Simultaneously down the hall, Rhoda was moving out of her office too. She was excited to pass the baton of intercession and church treasury. The prayer team was strong and powerful. She's witnessed countless miracles over the years. She especially loved the youth because they kept it real. They would make bold prayers and declarations that raised the faith of all who heard them. 100% of the intercessors she trained were exactly who they set out to be. Her favorite mentee, Dudley Harris is a praying young man. He joined the team at just 18 and now at 30 is an anesthesiologist. Dudley has absolutely no school debt because as he prayed, he also prepared. Rhoda read through cards, notes, and praise reports with tears in her eyes. Every sick person wasn't healed, every marriage wasn't saved, every desire wasn't met but Rhoda knew she served well. Rhoda allowed herself one file box of keepsakes as there were too many to keep. Just when she was looking to leave, Ryan knocked on her office door. "How you doing, mom?" Ryan asked. With tears of joy in her eyes, she turned to him and responded, "Good son, we did what we set out to do." Ryan teared up and agreed. Reaching out to hug her, Ryan thanked her for all her hard work, dedication, time, advice, and love. "We couldn't have done this without you! I haven't always done the right thing but Blake is the best part of me." Ryan spoke softly. Rhoda was deeply grateful that they were leaving ministry in wholeness and not in pieces. They'd taken some devastating blows but they had much to be grateful for. "Can I take you to lunch?" Ryan asked. "Absolutely," Rhoda replied. Rhoda got into the car with Ryan and left hers in the church parking lot after Ryan packed her trunk. They decided to head to *Milk & Honey*, one of Rhoda's favorite spots. When they arrived at the restaurant Rhoda greeted the shift manager who told her to just fill out an application because she was there more than him. The waitress escorted Rhoda and Ryan to her favorite table and took their drink orders. Ryan decided to order the crab hash and Rhoda decided on the lobster and grits. For the following hour they talked about Ryan's plans for the family and his struggles with Bradley's death. Rhoda aired her grievances with him since they were alone and he promised to work on himself. Ryan knew that momma Ro always had his best interests at heart but she didn't play about her daughter. Ryan listened as Rhoda gave him examples of things Blake dealt with at GLC that Ryan knew nothing of. He fell in love with his wife all over again just listened to the lengths Blake had gone, to preserve his name and character. Rhoda also informed him about an incident between Bradley and the daughter of a family who had long left the church. Ryan was shocked to hear about it and how Blake handled what happened. Rhoda told Ryan it was all he could handle in one day but over the years she would share the things Blake spared him from so he could study and travel. When Blake called Ryan during the meal, he told her he was on a date with his girl-friend. "Tell mom to give you the blue bag that I left in her backseat," Blake responded before ending their call. "She knows better than that and so do you. I told her that I was going to lunch with you because I cancelled lunch with her." Rhoda added. "I'm your favorite, huh?" Ryan teased. "You're my favorite *son,*" Rhoda responded. Before leaving, the manager teased Rhoda by handing her an application. She kept it for a young man at the church who needed a summer job. When Ryan pulled back up to GLC, Rhoda gave him the blue bag before heading home. When she saw Ryan begin a conversation with Deacon Vaughn and sister Jan, Rhoda told them Ryan had to go home and watched as he got into his car and drove away. Ryan was thankful that Rhoda kept him on track, they'd have to pull on Pastor Kemp moving forward.

6

PASSING THE BATON

*G*LC was packed to capacity for the ordination of Pastor Jason Demetrius Kemp. Family and friends from all over the country assembled to witness the momentous occasion. Apostle Sands would perform the ordination though Jason's direct leadership would come from his father, Bishop David Kemp Sr. Blake made the program so Lady Celestine could relax. On the platform sat Ryan and Blake, Apostle Sands and Grandma Ellie and Bishop Kemp and Lady Celestine. Many of Jason's friends assembled to support him including his best friend Trey and his wife Milly, Trey's brother Lucas and their mother Betty who decades prior attended Bishop Kemp's church. Jason's cousin Remy who was a comedy show on wheels and even David Kemp Jr., Jason's estranged brother. Seated with Shaye's parents, Harold and Darlene Wilkins were their twins Janiya and Jason Jr. There were 14 sets of twins born into GLC and one of Ryan's hecklers called it Good Lovin Church. Telling people not to attend or drink the water if they didn't want multiples. Oddly, enough people came hoping to have multiples. The service began with opening songs from the worship team as Jason and Shaye were escorted to their seats on the front row. Under Jason's headship the team had just released their first album. Jason stood to sing along from his seat and dance. When worship was over, Ryan and Blake stepped to the podium to share their hopes for GLC and their expectations for Jason and Shaye. A standing ovation ensued as Ryan and Blake gladly handed over the reins. Ryan spoke of the first time he and Jason met. Jason's eyes flooded with tears remembering the circumstances that brought them together. Jason honored Ryan for being a man of God not afraid to attach his name to his, amid a church scandal. He was also grateful for the Hairstons' for helping him to get Shaye back, after his mistakes. Blake spoke highly of Dr. Shaye and how she embodied the class and dignity necessary to stand beside her husband to build the people. "You're a woman already called to heal the physical body and I have no doubt that you're called to do it spiritually," said Blake. Shaye loved her some Blake Hairston and was honored to be a recipient of her advice, mentorship, and sisterhood. Blake had a way of entering your life from a higher rung on the ladder and before you realize it, she's pulled you up beside her. She and Blake were truly friends and Shaye was grateful for it. After their kind tribute Jason and Shaye hugged the Hairstons' before trading seats with them. Blake thought it was a great idea for the congregation to see a visual representation of the exchange of power. As Ryan and Blake sat on the front row, they could feel the weight and responsibility of their assignments lift off of them. Just the same, when Jason and Shaye sat on the platform the weight and responsibility of their assignment descended upon them. Ryan expected a greater glory to follow Jason as much has been given to him. The next speaker was listed as a surprise on the program and was none other than Jason's former bodyguard Lasso. Jason was wrecked when he saw him. Lasso told his story of being saved by the Nation of Islam and how he too had become a righteous man. Without embarrassing Jason, Lasso spoke of the day he called Lady Celestine because Jason had gone too far. Jason shook his head in agreement. "It was time to stop being your friend and be your big brother," Lasso spoke. He told Jason he was now Brother Lloyd X and offered Jason his righteous friendship and support. Everyone was moved by Brother Lloyd's words and he and Jason agreed to be friends and brothers for life. Before he sat down, Jason asked Brother Lloyd if he was FOI and he was. Before Jason could ask him about heading his security detail, Brother Llyod told him he didn't even have to ask. "I got you," Brother Lloyd assured him. Before Jason sat down, he blew kisses to Blake mouthing "Thank you." Blake mouthed "You're welcome," and was glad Brother Lloyd was easy to find. The worship team sang a couple songs before Lady Celestine and Bishop Kemp spoke. They encouraged their son to remain sober in his seat as pastor and not allow the intoxication of people's dependence on him to go to his head. "There are people whose belief in you is blind. They become open books and give you access to everything. Make sure you don't misuse their trust and teach them that you're not God," Bishop spoke. "Equip God's people to see Him inside of themselves and shun from becoming their mediator. They don't need *you* to speak to God on their behalf for they are individual pieces of Him," Bishop added. Amens could be heard throughout the sanctuary and Ryan wondered where Bishop Kemp was when people came to him for everything. Lady Celestine, dressed to kill in a blush ST. John knit skirt set with matching Tom Ford pumps, told Shaye to always be a lady. "When the dirty preachers smile in my son's face and offer you their hotel key, be a lady. When those heifers show up trying to steal your man, be a lady. When those no-good jokers who receive your help turn around and stab your back, be a lady and when they speak evil against you and accuse you of wrong-doing, be a lady," Lady C preached. "Be a Lady" people shouted. Blake stood with her hands in the air on all the above shouting "Let em' know Lady C." Ryan turned to Blake and asked how many people offered her their room key. "Dozens," Blake responded. "I need a list tonight, I ain't nobody's pastor," Ryan warned. Blake shook her head as people were still riled up from Lady Celestine's words. Jason jumped up and came to the mic to announce "Our first women's conference will be this fall entitled: Be a Lady" the congregation shouted. Shaye added, "with guest speakers Lady C Kemp and Lady B Hairston." Blake mouthed to Shaye "no ma'am I'm booked" as they shared a private laugh. Whenever they wanted intimate time with their husbands and someone asked them to do something, they always told people they were booked that weekend. They also mouthed to each other "Be victorious" which was code for put on that Victoria's Secret. Jason and Ryan just assumed that Blake and Shaye were always encouraging each other, in the Lord. After the commotion Apostle Sands and Grandma Ellie walked to the platform to ordain Jason as Pastor. With wisdom dripping off of him like honey, Apostle spoke about Jason's charge. Jason and Shaye had spent a few days with them speaking about what Jason's assignment was. Apostle talked about the day he met Jason and the restoration process he submitted himself to. Apostle thought it was fitting that Ryan was stepping aside to allow Jason to minister on his own terms. "My generation can learn a thing or two from you young men. So many raise successors to be a carbon copy of themselves. Ryan thought it not robbery to mentor Jason to exceed his own work," Apostle explained. "Amen" Ryan added. Apostle opened the book and extracted one sentence: *Preach the Word*. "You don't have to worry about people misquoting you if you, preach the word. You don't have to defend yourself if you preach the word. You don't have to walk the floor at night if you preach the word and you don't have to babysit the arrested development of others if you preach the word." Apostle exclaimed. "You say you're equipping the saints to find God within themselves and not somewhere in the sky and I told you to be prepared for empty seats." Apostle explained. "People who like their God mysterious and their hopes and dreams decades into the future, can't handle that kind of gospel," he added. "That would put the responsibility of living life more abundantly upon themselves. That would mean God, being able to do exceeding, abundantly above all that we ask or think, would be only according to the power that works within us," Apostle preached. Ryan and Bishop Kemp stood to their feet. "Jason will have empty seats because he's attempting to make God's people believe the scriptures! It's revolutionary," Apostle shouted. Ryan paced the floor knowing the hardest part of the job was getting so called Christians to follow the principles Jesus himself exemplified. "Massa gave you hope deferred, pie in the sky, sweet by and by Jesus to get you complacent with your circumstances. One day maybe God will, is not the message of the Kingdom. It's the message given to an economically disadvantaged race to stay in their place," Apostle ended. The businessmen in the congregation began to shout. "You all are still fighting my granddaddy's devil. This is not about our rights as foundational Black Americans, this is about our economic annihilation if we don't come out of our prayer closets and do for ourselves." Apostle closed his notes. While people were still shouting, he had the platform guests stand behind the Kemps including Ryan and Blake. Apostle laid his hands on Jason's head: "By the power invested in me before this world began, I confirm that you Jason Demetrius Kemp are a pastor in God's church. Raised up for this time and hour to prepare a people for an economic and theological shift. Preach and teach the word secondarily to your assignment as husband and father. Build a community of leaders who are self-sufficient in the here and now that a well done will be given of the Master." Apostle spoke. He then laid his hands on Shaye's head: "Dr. Shaye Latrice Kemp, I confirm that you are a First Lady and Intercessor in God's church. Raised up for this hour and time to assist your husband and pastor, to equip the saints. I charge you to be a sober wife and a godly mother first and the Lady of this house secondarily." Apostle concluded. As he presented Jason with his certificate and a gift from himself and Grandma Ellie. GLC I present to you, your Pastor and First Lady, Jason, and Dr. Shaye Kemp. The congregation applauded and cheered. Ryan and Blake wanted to dance a jig. As the service was about to end, everyone was asked to be seated for a special musical tribute. An acoustic guitar began to strum before Jason and Shaye's friend Shane appeared. Overwhelmed by his presence, they both began to cry. Shane had traveled from Dalkey, Ireland. Lady C grabbed the mic as he played to minister the acoustic version of *Touch the Sky* by Hillsong Worship. Jason was wrecked when she sang the words "*I got so high to fall so far but I found heaven is love, swept low.*" It reminded him of his road to ministry through the peaks and valleys of stardom. The congregation sang along "*My heart beating, my soul breathing I found my life, when I laid it down*". At the reception, Ryan and Blake presented Jason and Shaye with a couple's spa day. As the founding pastor of the church, the bylaws included that Ryan and Blake would receive 10% of the church's revenue for life. Ryan choose the monthly option as their additional income. While people ate and fellowshipped Blake and Ryan made their rounds before slipping out to go home. Blake hung out the moonroof on a wooded street by the house yelling "Wooohooo!" Ryan told Blake he had dibs next time. When they made it home, they still had 2 hours before Rhoda was scheduled to drop off the kids so they raced to the bedroom, leaving their clothes behind on the way.

Ryan sat in his office at *Taylor Made* working on the plans for a new nursing home when he received a call from Dr. Ethan.

After almost 10 weeks in a coma, Jenna has awakened. Ryan told Ethan he was grateful that she pulled through. Ethan told Ryan that Jenna is severely brain damaged and will require life-long care. Ryan offered his empathy. Dr. Worthington went on to say the baby would be delivered in a few hours at just 26 weeks. Ryan asked Ethan if he should come but Ethan told him, no. He told Ryan he would send pictures and also let him know the baby is a girl. Ryan told Ethan he looked forward to seeing her and congratulated Ethan on grandparenthood. When Ryan ended the call, he immediately called Blake to bring her up to speed. Blake thought it was odd for them to just find out the baby is a girl. "Do you think they assume the baby isn't Bradley's?" Blake inquired. "I feel horrible for all they've been through but I pray this baby isn't. We've been through enough to also be the grandparents of 2 children from 2 mom's," Ryan added. "We? I'm not a grandma either way, you and Brooke are grandparents," Blake said frankly. "Don't play with me woman," Ryan added but Blake was so serious. Ryan asked if she wanted him to pick up dinner and Blake agreed. Ryan wanted to talk slick but there was an echo in his office and Lawson was seeing clients. He told Blake she was fortunate that there were people around or he'd say what was on his mind. She told him to text it before ending the call. When the message came though she received a peach, a splash, and an eggplant. She sent back the emoji with a headache and he replied with the emoji for Taurus and the emoji for poop. After laughing at Ryan's response Blake went back to her task. The children were off from school and she was home preparing the treat bags for Royce's 6th birthday and the twin's 10th birthday. Their birthdays were only a few days apart and she only had the energy to have them on the same day. Royce was having a shark theme; Ryan Jr. wanted a disco theme and Rayne wanted a spa theme. Since the twins were the opposite sex, Blake allowed them to have separate parties. The upcoming Saturday Royce's party was from 2pm-4pm in the loft, Ryan Jr.'s party was from 6pm-8pm in the backyard with Ryan and Josh as hosts and Rayne's party was also from 6pm-8pm in the basement with Blake and Lexi as hosts.

Miles away Gavin, Evans and Freddie were playing cards and planning to go to the pier, to clean up their boat for spring fishing. Years ago, they came together to invest in the boat when Lawson had one for sale. Each year they would fish, hang out or enjoy the boat separately. The prior summer Evans and Rhoda took the boat on a trip to the Newport Jazz Festival in Rhode Island. Gavin would sometimes sail to Hampton to visit Pat and Parrish and sometimes Freddie would entertain company. They each earned their Captain's license after spending so much money to hire one. It was a great way to spend time away from the hustle and bustle of the DMV. The men spent their days laughing and making fun of each other and today was no exception. Gavin told the men about Blake's visits and the day Ryan came banging on the door looking for her boyfriend. Evans was glad to see Ryan shook if only for a moment. Gavin shared with the men how Lilly was bold as a bat until the first lady walked in the door. Freddie told Gavin he and Evans were glad he was alive. "Three more performances and you'd be dead," Freddie joked. The men fell out laughing together and banging on the table. The doorbell rang and it was the food they had delivered from the rib joint. Gavin loved living alone and the peace to do as he pleased. He was right around the corner from Joshua and Bella if he needed them and it felt so good. Gavin considered buying the house from Blake and Ryan, if he could convince them to lower the price a bit. Meanwhile on a secluded street in DC, Ryan sat in his Mercedes smoking a cigar and drinking a shorty of cognac. Since Bradley's death he's been drinking daily and smoking cigars is a new habit. The weight of all that he's responsible for and the pain of Bradley's death, was enough to make him insane. Each day he would sit somewhere quiet and gain his peace. He hoped and prayed Jenna's baby didn't belong to Bradley and he prayed that Tia's baby did. He knew she was young but having a piece of Bradley wrapped in a new beginning would be nice. When he got back to the firm, he went into his private bathroom to brush his teeth, change his shirt and finish the last half of his day.

It was Saturday afternoon and the Hairston residence was bustling with party preparations. Lexi had converted all three areas into the children's dream parties. Royce and his 8 guests played pin the tail on the donkey, had their faces painted and did the Dino dance. Rhoda made him a shirt that read "6 and so fine" with her crafting machine. Royce had a ball! The children dined on the fine cuisine of cheeseburger sliders, tater tots, strawberry popcorn, ice cream and cake. To top off his special day, a dinosaur came to the party and made balloon animals. The children left with the parting gifts of Royce's favorite boardgame, books and bubbles. In the break between his party and his older siblings, Royce begged to attend Ryan Jr.'s disco. After a few promises and $30 in bribes, Ryan told Royce he could come but that he had to stay in the far corner of the yard. Royce was so excited. In the basement were 6 pedicure stations and 6 nail stations. Rayne, dressed in a pink tracksuit and flip flops awaited her 11 guests including her cousin Brielle: with the remaining guests from school, church, or dance class. The girls would split up in 2 groups for pedicures or manicures then would switch. They had their choice of designs and colors. Once their nails were finished, Lexi had a station for them to get their makeup done or their hair decorated with accessories. Rayne requested that her menu included crab cake sandwiches, salad, and fruit. Lexi also included chicken salad croissants and flatbread pizza. Rhoda made a t-shirt for Rayne which she wore under her tracksuit that read "10 with rich girl tendencies." The spa party was in full swing. The girls receiving pedicures sipped on punch in plastic wine glasses with sugar around the rim. The girls getting their nails done sat in chairs with massage mats. Lexi and Blake were laughing in the corner because Rayne's friend Ciara from ballet class asked the technician for a fill-in on her full set of nails. The technician had the supplies so she did the full set and Blake paid the difference. When Ryan crashed the party to see which girls were too grown for her age, he immediately picked Ciara. He told Blake that Rayne couldn't be friends with her or the little girl Desi who came wearing false eyelashes. Rayne had a great time and received some cool gifts. Each girl left with a backpack filled with snacks and age appropriate cosmetics.At the same time in the backyard, Ryan Jr.'s party was lit. His cousins: Paris Jr, Pierre and Joshua Jr. as well has his friends from church, school and soccer were in attendance. The boys had practiced a group dance over zoom to perform at the party. The crowd of rowdy 10-year-old boys hung together in groups and ignored the girls invited to the party. Since Ryan Jr.'s party was coed a few of the parents stayed. Rhoda made Ryan Jr.'s birthday shirt and it read "10 and turned up" since their dance routine was performed to the clean version of Turn Down for What by DJ Snake and Lil John. Lexi hired a DJ and a dance floor was laid over the grass. Royce was jumping in the corner just happy to be invited when the boys performed their dance. Ryan recorded it on his phone as did some of the parents. The girls watched from the party tables and ate tacos and virgin margaritas. Lexi had a local Mexican restaurant cater the food and lined up the items on a concession stand made from a cardboard food truck. Ryan Jr. wanted video game trucks but Ryan knew that would exceed his 2-hour time slot and said no. By the end of the party the boys were sweaty and the girls were bored. The men laughed knowing it wouldn't always be that way. Ryan Jr.'s party went on until 9:30 but Rayne and Royce didn't care. By 10:30 everyone was gone and the Hairston home was spotless. That night Blake and Ryan laid in the bed discussing the parties and informing each other of the gossip they heard from the parents. Lexi had the best tea of all but Blake kept it to herself, knowing it would be a shock to many. Victoria was next door at Barbara Edwards house preparing the nursery for Tia's baby. The two women ooh'd and ahhh'd at the tiny items. Sharing stories about their children and grandchildren brought such joy to their hearts. Tia successfully finished treatment and was intent on making sure her and Bradley's child was healthy. Barbara explained to Tia that the Hairstons' requested a paternity test because drugs were involved but believed Tia, that Bradley was the only one. Victoria knew in her heart as well that Tia was a good girl and was thankful to be next door to the baby. Monica, the sponsor assigned to Tia's sobriety allowed Barbara to tell her about Bradley's passing while in treatment. Monica was able to explain to Tia that horrible things may happen in life but her response to those occurrences were in her own power. Tia admitted to only doing the drugs to be accepted by Bradley and often felt sick because of them. Barbara's son Rashaad was Tia's father. Rashaad was in the military and as a single father he couldn't provide the stability Tia needed because they moved so much, so Tia stayed with Barbara to grow some roots. Rashaad was sorely disappointed that Tia was a teen mom and addicted to drugs and blamed himself for not giving her "the talk." Tia's mom Teresa was a rebellious teen and had 3 children by the time she was 19. When Rashaad met her, she lied about her children being her niece and nephews and didn't know otherwise until she was pregnant with Tia. Since breaking up with Teresa and gaining sole custody of Tia, Rashaad has recently discovered, Teresa had 4 more children. Tia used the money her father sent for the past 2 months to buy things for the baby. She was excited to have a piece of Bradley and was overjoyed to learn the baby is a boy.Ryan was on his way to the *Litter Box*, to meet with the owner as a potential client. Business was booming and owner Mark Lyles, was looking to expand the club's blueprint. Ryan hadn't been to a strip club since he and Devin's days in undergrad but it came with the territory. When Ryan arrived, the owner greeted him and claimed to be a fan. Taken aback, Ryan thanked him and walked inside the club. For the following 3 hours, Mark gave Ryan a guided tour of the club and his vision for expansion. Ryan offered some suggestions based on the current layout and pointed out what areas the city would flag. Mark was impressed with Ryan's expertise and warnings. The club was packed to capacity with the afterwork crowd. Ryan was amazed how many people patronized the club on a Tuesday night. For over a decade he taught Tuesday night bible study and there was no comparison in crowd size. The women hung from the ceiling and put on full performances. It was a far cry from the lackluster talent in Wilberforce, OH. After the tour, Mark brought Ryan to his private booth overlooking the entire club to discuss numbers. Ryan pulled out his laptop and went to work. When Ryan printed out his bid, it wasn't the cheapest or the most expensive but nicely in the middle. Ryan broke down the reason for his price line by line, explaining the details necessary to scale the club within building codes. Mark asked Ryan if he could sleep on it, Ryan responded that he could put a week on it. "You can take about a week to decide because I actually have 2 projects ahead of yours and wouldn't be able to draw them until then," Ryan explained. Mark appreciated Ryan's indifference and offered him a drink. Ryan accepted. Just then a cocktail waitress wearing pasties and a schoolgirl uniform took his order. In addition to his drink Ryan ordered some sliders and coleslaw. Mark had a full-on menu with master chefs preparing the food. During food and drinks, Mark told Ryan he was welcome to stop by anytime offering his private booth for food and drinks or a private dance. "I offer all of my special guests the utmost discretion and a private entrance," Mark added. Ryan agreed to take him up on his offer. Ryan Jr. put him on blast saying his car smelled like smoke. Thankfully, it was the day after picking up pit BBQ, so Blake thought nothing of it. Ryan would be able to drink and smoke in peace. "Okay Rev just let me know you're coming and I will hook you up," Mark said. "I don't pastor anymore," Ryan countered. "Man, that doesn't matter one bit, you'll find out just as my grandfather and father did that the Lord never stops using you," Mark explained. Ryan was intrigued to know how the grandson and son of preachers, ends up owning a thriving strip club. "It's not just me, many of my dancers are PKs. I've seen so much in church that I would rather be upfront with mines," Mark added. "Respect" Ryan said and gave him a pound. Ryan stood to leave and looked out over the club before leaving and saw Lilly twirling a ribbon and gyrating in a tutu. Laughing out loud, Ryan realized Gavin had strange taste. The following morning Ryan dropped his car off at the detailers to rid it of smoke and any trace of his lunch break routine. Lawson picked him up, on his way to the firm. When Ryan checked his email, he had a voicemail from Mark telling him he won the bid. Ryan emailed him his acceptance letter and sent Mark his bill. Ryan also included the date the blueprints would be finished and always delivered 3 days before the date on the contract. By lunchtime, the detailer called and told Ryan his car was ready. Since Lawson had a client and Taylor was in the field, Ryan ordered a ride from an app. While driving back to the office he received a call from Blake asking where he was because she was at his office with lunch. Ryan told Blake he was getting gas but would soon arrive. First pulling over to a gas station to fill his tank, Ryan made his way back to the firm. When he arrived in the lot, he asked Blake to come outside and eat in his car. When she climbed inside wearing a mini dress, stilettos, and his favorite lipstick he was pleasantly surprised. After a passionate kiss, he started rubbing her upper thighs while she removed his food from a straw handled basket. She handed him an over-stuffed roast beef sandwich from his favorite deli. Ryan flirted with his wife just to see her smile before eating his food. "You smell incredible," Ryan added. "Thank you, daddy," Blake replied. Blake loved when Ryan complimented her fragrances. Though she wore them for herself she appreciated him loving them too. "What you wearing? Put daddy down with the new-new," Ryan spoke. "It's not new but I'm wearing *Nouez Moi* by House of Sillage. Ryan loved the way Blake took care of herself and represented him in the world. "You make me proud, Bae" Ryan added. Blake smiled and thanked him. The couple ate their food and Ryan talked greasy as usual. Planning to receive his Wednesday night Willy as Ryan had just named it, Blake was escorted to her car. After Ryan shut her door and kissed her eyelids, Blake left to get the children from school.When Ryan got back to his desk, he realized he left his cell phone in his car and went back outside to get it. When he got back inside, he saw 2 missed calls. One from Dr. Worthington and another from a number he didn't recognize. Both calls had voicemails, so Ryan first listened to the call attached to the unknown number. As he listened to the call tears streamed from his eyes. Grateful for answered prayer, it was the lab in Virginia calling to confirm that Bradley is not the father of Jenna's baby. Ryan texted Blake writing that Bradley is not the father!!!!!!! Ryan listened to Dr. Ethan's message. He thanked Ryan for his support and friendship throughout the whole ordeal. Telling Ryan, he restored his faith and hope. Ryan sobbed listening to Ethan's kind words. "I guess you probably heard by now, the baby isn't Bradley's but in fact belongs to Jerome Headley Jr." Ethan explained. "My wife named her because Jenna can no longer write or speak. She named our granddaughter Miracle Ann Worthington," Ethan said proudly. "We will call her Miry Ann," Ethan added. Blake called Ryan's desk phone so they celebrated together. Ryan told her who the baby belonged to and her rather urban name. Blake was tickled about the play on Mary Ann and agreed that she would've expected the name Grace or Faith from the Worthingtons' but had to admit she is a miracle.

Ryan was lit! For the 4th Thursday in a row he was at the *Litter Box* turned up. Surrounded by dancers and inebriated from Cognac, he was dancing up a storm. As they chanted "Go Ryan, Go Ryan!" He was grooving to a song in his own head because the dancer on stage was performing a routine to a slow song. When he was finished the ladies crowded around him for counseling. He had already convinced Misty to leave her abusive relationship. Bambi registered for summer school to become a nursing assistant and Black Hawk took her children back from her grandmother. It was Candy's turn and she felt obligated to wait for Tyrone to get out of jail in 22 years. With slurred speech, Ryan told Candy to move on. "Only a selfish man would allow you to place your life on hold because his is," Ryan explained. Ryan told Candy to use her money to start her consulting business since she was an expert at branding. She had successfully become the Litter Box's premier dancer. There were desserts on the menu bearing her name including Ryan's favorite: Candy's Box: a chewy brownie with a molten fudge center with a scoop of ice cream, a cocktail, a song performed by an A list rapper and an adult candy bonanza that sells out every Halloween. The girls agreed that was a great idea and Candy felt good about it too. Later that evening Ryan was too drunk to drive. Mark was off but his business partner Mike, told Ryan he was going to call his ride. Ryan agreed not knowing who Mike was calling and proceeded to drink. As he looked over the crowd from the private balcony his eyes fixated on the crowd. Struggling to believe what he was seeing; he began to squint. Blinking time and time again, he stood up to lean over the ledge. Realizing his mind wasn't playing tricks on him, his jaw dropped as he saw a couple kissing, rubbing on one another and in the heat of passion; none other than Nia and Brooke. Ryan took out his camera to record them and couldn't believe his eye. How long had they been at it? Ryan thought. Just then someone grabbed him on the shoulder. He turned around and it was Mr. Blake Evans. Evans told Ryan it was time to go but Ryan pointed down to Nia and Brooke. "That's old, why do you think they're both divorced?" Evans said dismissingly. He escorted Ryan to his own car and helped him into the passenger seat. Never asking how Evans arrived at the club Ryan began to throw up. Evans handed him a hoodie from his back seat as there was nothing else in the car. When Mike saw what was happening from the back door, he shouted to Evans to wait one minute. A cocktail waitress handed Evans 2 champagne buckets lined in plastic. Evans handed her a hundred-dollar bill and got back into the car. He handed Ryan the buckets and turned the ignition to leave. When the two men arrived at Evans and Rhoda's house, Evans escorted Ryan down to his mancave to take a shower and change his clothes. Rhoda was over Vivian's so it was the perfect time to bring Ryan inside. Outside, Freddie parked Evans car in the driveway and got into the car with his lady friend and she pulled away. After his shower, Evans bagged up Ryan's clothes for the trash and called Blake. When Blake answered, Evans told her that Ryan had stopped by to talk and fell asleep and he wasn't going to wake him up. Blake thanked her Dad for calling and locked the house and armed the security system while he was on the phone. Ryan slept his liquor off and woke up the following morning with a splitting headache. To sober him up, Evans gave him another drink. He told Ryan that he called Blake and told him what he said. Ryan was so grateful to Evans and thanked him for his grace. "It's the least I can do since I have my own vices, son" Evans said in comfort. Ryan took another shower before heading home. He texted his partners to inform them he'd be working from his home office. When he got upstairs Rhoda was in the kitchen cooking breakfast. She turned to Ryan and asked how he wanted his eggs. "Scrambled with cheddar cheese," he replied. He could tell by her conversation she was speaking to Blake and sat in silence. When Rhoda handed Ryan his plate, he smiled and thanked her. Shortly after Rhoda ended her call and she and Evans sat opposite Ryan to eat their breakfast. "I'm sorry mom," Ryan offered. "Baby, you've been in ministry the entire time most people are figuring out who they are, that kind of pressure catches up to everyone; Add on your responsibilities and your recent loss, thank God it was just liquor," Rhoda said in a motherly tone. "You're gonna go home and be with your family and it's water under the bridge. If Blake finds out its because you told her." Rhoda finished. Ryan thanked her and Evans and loved them all the more.

7

PERFECT LOVE

*W*eeks later, Blake walked into her office suite adjacent to Shaye's private practice for the first time in months. She was long overdue for her first session with her new mentees. Each year, Blake chose a small group of women to mentor for 18 months. The air was becoming stale as May gave way to June. Blake loathed the summer months and kept herself busy so they'd fly by. Dressed in a hot pink ruffled jumpsuit with side cut outs, matching *Hermès Oran* sandals and the design house's *Rose Indien* lipstick; Blake was summer ready. Climbing out of Ryan's new *Mercedes S 560 Coupe* in the beautiful shade of Selenite Grey. Paris was always enticing Ryan with new stock but Blake new it signified a fresh start. Ryan usually wouldn't allow her to drive his new ride so soon but her *Bentayga* needed scheduled maintenance that same morning. When Blake walked through the door into the reception area, her new receptionist Isla, greeted her. Isla was a local high school student who earned volunteer credits for working with Blake or Shaye on weekends. Blake walked down the hall with her Birkin in the crook of her left arm, while pulling her roller brief with her right. When she opened the door to the meeting room a crowd yelled "Surprise!" Standing before Blake were her 5 new mentees accompanied by Shaye, Ava, Micah, and Jewel. Overcome with gratitude she began to cry. The room had been transformed into a brunch in her honor. Coincidently she matched the hot pink and orange themed room. "You are appreciated" hung on a banner behind 4 easels each made by her previous mentees. Blake hugged all 9 women and wept with joy. Micah placed a tiara on Blake's head and told her it represented the hundreds of crowns she has placed, fixed, or repaired on the heads of other women. The new mentees: Patrice, Kylie, Dawn, Kenzie, and Joi were excited to learn and grow. Jewel put on some music and invited everyone to make their plates after serving Blake. The surprise brunch included French toast, apple and sage sausage, mini quiche, crispy breakfast potatoes, crab balls, seafood pasta salad, fruit, mango tea and strawberry limeade. The sweets table contained brownies, blondies, and assorted tarts. While everyone ate, each of Blake's former mentees shared their experience in the program. They were all transparent and relatable so the new mentees understood that the circle was tight and confidential. Shaye, Ava, Jewel, and Micah presented Blake with a pair of YSL opium sandals to signify that Blake doesn't teach you to walk in her shoes but gives you the tools to walk in your own. Blake was blessed by their words and appreciation and told the new ladies why she was proud of each former mentee. "Ava found her identity, Jewel found her purpose, Micah found her worth and Shaye found her voice." Blake explained. I am extremely thankful to be part of your journeys and thank you for trusting me with your areas of opportunity," Blake concluded. After cleaning up the decorations and trash, the former mentees left a small tray of treats before excusing themselves to leave. Blake called the meeting to order and reached into her roller brief for their assessment exercises. Giving each woman a white box with a lid, she gave them glue, gems, markers, stickers, and colorful art supplies to decorate them. Each woman selected her items from the middle of the table and began to decorate her box. Blake set her timer for 30 minutes and watched them work. They spoke among themselves and laughed as they decorated the boxes. Blake observed them and jotted down notes concerning them. When the timer went off, Blake gave each woman 5 pieces of scratch paper. She instructed them to talk among themselves and come up with 5 reasons why she chose them for the current cycle of the program. She gave them another 30 minutes but this time she left the room. During the exercise the women shared their stories about how they met Blake. They shared their challenges, pains, disappointments, and let downs. When Blake returned to the room, she asked them for their 5 reasons why they believe she chose them. Appointing Patrice as their representative the list was presented to Blake. "After discussing various topics, we came up with the following," Patrice spoke:

1. We grew up in single parent homes
2. We survived an abusive relationship whether physically, verbally, or mentally
3. We are the black sheep of our families
4. We love hard and wear our hearts on our sleeves
5. We live paycheck to paycheck

Patrice concluded. Blake wrote some notes and asked each woman why she chose to decorate her box as she did. Patrice told Blake she used jewels because she has expensive taste and likes glamorous things. Joi told Blake she used feathers because she likes textures and described herself as creative. Kenzie told Blake she chose all the yellow decorations because she's positive, happy and looks on the bright side. Dawn told Blake she used jewels, feathers, and bright colors because she is bold and takes pride in her appearance. Kylie told Blake she used pearls and white feathers because she's into luxury and glamour. Blake thanked them for their participation and gave them their assessments. "I asked you to decorate the boxes because I knew they would show me the façade you offer to the world around you. Each of you go out of your way to appear one way in front of others but on the inside, you're steeping in the anger from an absent father or the fear from an absent mother," Blake offered. "You cover the rejection of physical, verbal and mental abuse with elaborate exteriors. To seem worthy amid broken family ties, you offer yourselves emotionally to other broken people and your self-worth is expressed in your financial irresponsibility," Blake continued. "I chose each and every one of you because you share the common thread of being leaders in the making but you bonded yourselves together with trauma," Blake concluded. Each woman had tears streaming down her face, recognizing her own skewed self-image. Appreciative that Blake saw something in each of them that they hadn't considered gave them hope. Dawn expressed to the group that she spent more time on her outward appearance than her inner confidence. Blake encouraged the group and shared how she only had 2 mentees who decorated the inner lid, signifying a high self-worth. She pointed out that they had met one of them which is Shaye. Blake told the women she believed in them and gave them journals to chart their growth. She asked each woman what she hoped to get out of the program and jotted their expectations down. She encouraged the women that they'd meet their goals if they were willing to do the work. She closed them out in prayer before bringing the session to a close. When Blake got into the car, she called Ryan. "How was your appreciation brunch?" he inquired. Blake told him it was beautiful remembering he chose her outfit and that's how she matched with the theme. She asked if he wanted her to pick up some dinner and Ryan teased Blake saying, "I already picked up something for dinner, so bring my baby girl back to the house." Ryan always named his cars after women but after 2 weeks still hadn't named his current automobile. Blake agreed and made her way through the notorious DMV traffic toward home.

When Ryan looked in the mail, he discovered an invitation to Tia's baby shower. The gender-neutral postcard listed Bradley's 18th birthday as it's date. Ryan's emotions began to stir thinking about the possibility of new life springing forth from such tragedy. He wanted the baby to have every opportunity for heath, happiness, and wholeness. Lost in his thoughts, Ryan didn't notice when Gavin walked up beside him. Startled when his father put on a strange voice, Gavin laughed when Ryan prepared to swing on him. "Boy I'll knock you out," Gavin said matter-of-factly. "I've been calling your name, why you out here daydreaming like a young boy in a brothel?" Gavin inquired. Disturbed by his father's example, Ryan asked what he did to be in the presence of such a great man, to be facetious. Gavin played like he was beating Ryan up in response. "I'm here because I want to purchase the house. Before you get all professional on me, I need you to know that your son took your mother for $25k and I need to replace it." Gavin said. "I owe 18 payments on the house which equals about $23k. I know I can get $500k for the house but I know that's out of your budget. Just pay the remaining payments and the taxes each year and keep your money," Ryan concluded. Gavin was thrilled to hear Ryan's offer and accepted it with joy. He only had $500k to his name. Now he could live out his years with dignity. He would give Victoria $25k, use $23K to pay off Ryan and Blake's house for letting him live there and leave money behind for his children and grandchildren. That evening Ryan told Blake what he did for Gavin. She asked when he started giving houses away before asking her for her agreement. He admitted to being emotional after reading the baby shower invitation. Blake looked at him with a blank stare since they agreed to sell the house months prior. Blake expressed to Ryan how Gavin should've had an exit strategy when leaving an over 40-year marriage. She also pointed out that the house would only go up in value if it keeps being updated but would decrease and become a liability over the course of Gavin's years left on earth. Ryan knew he made a mistake as it was him who taught Blake how to move money around. He apologized to his wife for acting independently of their covenant. He knew he had to fix it. Ryan called his father. When Gavin answered he sounded like he won the lottery. Ryan expressed to Gavin that he didn't have Blake's agreement to not sell the house and had to take back his offer. "I had just received the invitation to Tia's baby shower and acted out of my emotions," he explained. Gavin sat in silence for a few moments and asked Ryan if he could stay for 18 months while still paying the mortgage, giving him time to find a condo or apartment to move into. Ryan asked Blake and she agreed. Gavin apologized for thinking it was okay to ask Ryan without Blake and wished them a good evening. Ryan was tired of messing up and wanted a drink and cigar.

8

NEW LIFE

*I*t was a sweltering summer afternoon when friends and family gathered to celebrate the life growing in Tia's womb. The room was decorated in yellows and greens in an alphabet block theme. Ryan and Blake attended the shower without the children, who were with Lexi and Paris. Tia looked beautiful in a white summer dress with yellow and green flowers woven into her braids. The baby was due in 7 weeks and people kept asking Tia what she was having. Barbara and Victoria are the only ones who know the gender because Tia requested that it be a surprise. When Tia saw Ryan and Blake, she walked over to greet them. Blake told her they were so excited and Ryan began to cry. Tia saw that his pain was raw like her own and cried in his arms. Victoria saw the scene playing out and she too became undone. Rhoda grabbed the microphone from the DJ and asked everyone to bow their heads in prayer. *"Heavenly Father, we've gathered together in your name to honor you for your goodness. Your mercy endures forever God and we give you all the praise! We thank you for our directed paths and delight in your righteous ways. We come to say thank you for new life and new beginnings God, we lift up Tia and thank you* *for her wholeness, we thank you for perfecting that which concerns her and binding up her aching heart. We thank you for the baby and his or her purpose in you. We ask that in this day you will surround us with peace. We aren't here to mourn Bradley Oh God but to celebrate his seed. I ask that hearts be merry and lifted and that you blow your healing winds in this place. We thank you that life has sprung forth, worthy of your favor and grace. We thank you for an atmosphere of love, harmony and compassion in Christ's name we pray, Amen."* Rhoda prayed. The DJ started to play music and the party was officially on. During the shower Rashaad and Ryan had a talk. They both agreed they could've done better for their children but Ryan assured Rashaad that if he is the grandfather, Tia would have his full support. The games began and Blake sat far in the back of the room to hide. She despised baby shower games and didn't want to be called upon. Rhoda won a large *All* detergent in the game, Winner Takes All. Many partygoers won gift cards to ice cream, coffee or take out establishments. Victoria and Barbara were pleased that everyone had a great time. Ryan asked his mother if Brooke was invited and she said yes. Blake noticed her absence but didn't think much about it. Tia was escorted to a seat that resembled a throne to open her gifts. For the next 2 hours everyone watched as tiny clothes and the newest baby gadgets were unwrapped. By early evening Blake and Ryan made their rounds before heading to get the children from Virginia. When they pulled onto the expressway Lexi called to ask if they could stay and Blake agreed. She and Ryan stopped off for some food before going in the house. Later that evening Blake was drying off from a long bath when she heard loud bangs and crashes coming from the lower level. She placed on her robe and descended the steps. Ryan was trashing the place! Yelling and crying at the same time, while punching holes in their walls. Afraid to approach him during his episode, Blake waited for him to wear himself out. Ryan's heart was racing as he struggled to breathe. His knuckles were bruised and his anger was raging. With his forehead pressed to the wall in the foyer, Blake tenderly wrapped her arms around his waist from behind. Just feeling her body pressed against his, made him calm. His breathing returned to normal and his anger turned into disappointment. As he turned around to face his gorgeous wife, tears streamed down his face. Blake wiped away his tears smelling the liquor on his breath. While she ran her hands through the thick waves on his head to soothe her hurting king, Ryan spoke "I need help B, I've been drinking every day since he died." Blake nodded her head in agreement and replied "Okay." The following morning, Ryan was still asleep when Blake went to the kitchen to cook breakfast. The heat index was high so she left the shades and blinds closed. Deciding to keep things light, she made a Greek omelet with spinach, tomato, feta, and red onion topped with her favorite olive tapenade from *Trader Joe*. Pairing her omelet with cold pressed watermelon juice, Blake sat down in the sunroom to enjoy her meal. She knew Ryan was taking Bradley's death hard but she had no idea he was drinking on a daily basis. With the move, taking care of the children, the church transition, mentoring and preparing for the Light Awards to go virtual, she didn't see the signs. One thing's for sure she didn't blame herself and trusted him to govern himself accordingly. While thinking things through, she decided to delegate some of her tasks to well abled mentees while walking with Ryan through sobriety. After she finished eating, she went to get her phone to text Lexi. When she got back to her master suite Ryan was still sleeping so she decided to let him rest. When she reached into her nightstand to recover her phone, she had over 30 text messages. Everyone from Rhoda to Anastasia had texted her. She opened the text from Lexi because she had her children. Blake's eyebrows almost touched her hairline when she saw the screenshot of Nia and Brooke wearing wedding dresses. The social media caption read: *After years of pretending, me and Bae have made it official. We decided to get married on my late son's birthday to cover my pain with love.* Followed by rainbow hearts and two women. Blake responded to Lexi: *well alrighty then, I will be there to get the kids by 11.* Lexi responded: *you can meet me at your parent's house around noon because I have to bring Aunt Ro some new sheets.* Blake responded with the thumbs up and texted the text acronym for talk to you later. Blake was surprised the two were married though Lexi had just told her during Rayne's party that they were an item. Blake read Rhoda's text concerning them and literally laughed out loud. Most people texted a photo from the wedding accompanied by a pair of eyes. Blake responded to them with her famous initials *IJWH* meaning I just work here. Blake put her phone back into the nightstand and kept it on silent. She went into her closet to find something to wear when she picked up the children in a few hours. She chose a baby blue romper and paired it with some Bottega Lido sandals in the color ice. While she was in her closet looking through her intimate's drawer Ryan crawled up behind her and licked the back of her thigh. Blake screamed and clunked him in the head with a shoe. He laid on the floor pretending to be hurt before pulling her on top of him. "Thanks for staying through all I've put you through," Ryan said. "You're welcome," Blake responded. "I reached out to the Blakemore House for treatment and someone already got back in touch, I go tomorrow to get started. My counselor will be Brice Fletcher and he's assigned to grief triggered alcohol abuse. Thursdays are the meetings for couples with a sober partner." Ryan explained. Blake assured Ryan that she would be present at each meeting and was proud that he knew to get help sooner than later. Blake told Ryan she would be picking up the children around noon and reminded him that he needed to put one of the pieces of artwork or a long mirror over the holes he punched in the wall until their handy man Diego comes to fix the wall. Ryan agreed and said he'd do it right away. He asked if she could make him a breakfast sandwich while he hung the mirror. Blake told him she would and headed downstairs to make it. Before she made it to the kitchen, she heard an expletive leave Ryan's mouth and knew he seen his phone. Since Brooke and Nia gained a measure of success separately in reality television and fashion, media outlets reported on their nuptials. For over a week, entertainment news was buzzing with different aspects of the wedding. One of Brooke's reality television friends Savannah was her matron of honor. The lead actress of a hit television show that Nia styled was her maid of honor. The elaborate ceremony was attended by friends with no family present except the children. Ryan was especially perturbed when Brooke cast herself as a grieving mother whose life was saved by Nia's love. Telling interviewers that she didn't want to live and found it impossible to face each day without Bradley. She told an internet podcast that the last time she saw her son before the accident was during a family breakfast where they spoke and laughed for hours. Brice told Ryan that Brooke's antagonism was a great opportunity for him to cope with his own grief without liquor. Encouraging Ryan to journal each day concerning his feelings, Brice provided him with new tools to cope. By Early September Ryan was transferred to grief counseling in place of AA meetings. It was there that he gained a new outlook on Bradley's death and the pain became bearable. With the support of many different demographics of grievers Ryan knew he wasn't alone. He met a woman who lost her child 30 years prior who had just given herself permission to grieve. There was a man who lost his child because he was an hour late picking her up from school and she was kidnapped on video just 7 minutes prior to his arrival. The man's grief was coupled with the fact that his daughter hadn't yet been found. It happened 12 years ago yet the man knew when 7 minutes had passed without watching a clock. "I had 53 minutes to become a better man," he spoke.

Ryan especially felt for the man because his pain was perpetual. The man stopped living over a decade ago and had truly been residing in hell.

On a hot September day at 3:16 in the afternoon Tia gave birth to a healthy baby boy who she named Tristan Michael Edwards. At 5 pounds and 3 ounces he came into the world, in beauty and wholeness. Barbara and Victoria never left her side. It was a momentous occasion and the family came to the hospital to see him. The doctors immediately performed the paternity test and it was sent to the lab in Virginia that had Bradley's DNA. When Ryan held the sweet baby boy, he knew he was a Hairston. Looking exactly like baby Royce Blake knew it too. The kids were excited to be uncles and an aunt. Rayne wanted a girl but loved him anyway. Though Victoria told her about the baby's birth, Brooke didn't visit or call. Tia had 2 years left of school and desired to go in person so Victoria and Barbara agreed to care for the baby during the day. Rashaad Face Timed from his base and took screenshots so he and Tristan could be in the same photo. Ryan texted pics of Tristin to Devin, Lawson, Tevin, Taylor, and Jason. Blake sent pics to Lexi and Lady Celestine. Everyone was excited and joyous which put Tia at ease. The real celebration arrived a few weeks later when it was confirmed that Bradley indeed was the father.

The Hairston's 15th wedding anniversary was coming up in October and the family inquired of their plans. They had been through so much over the years that they wanted to keep things low key. Rhoda offered to watch the children if they desired to travel but Blake and Ryan weren't sure. Ryan asked Blake if she was interested in renewing their vows and having a reception at home. He thought it would be a great time for a fresh start.

Blake agreed but told him it had to be small and intimate. Deciding to include 50 people or less, they began making plans. Everyone was excited and jumped right on board. Ryan and Blake agreed to have Jason officiate the ceremony and to hire a local children's orchestra to play. The backyard would be transformed into a flower garden and a tent would be erected for dinner and dancing. Their actual anniversary would fall of a Friday night so they planned the wedding for that very evening. Blake chose cream, burnt orange, gold, and chocolate to incorporate autumn into their celebration. It was her favorite season as she was both married and born in October. She and her good girlfriend Ardena both had that in common though the dates were different. They added special touches to the ceremony and reception to honor their village. So many people stood alongside them over the years to keep their family supported, especially family. The couple ordered a special plaque for Rhoda who is literally the glue of their family. Her support in ministry and in their lives is incomparable. The couple also chose to present gifts to Nia, Paris, Bella, and Joshua for their support as well. The invitations were mailed and everything was set for their autumn vowel renewal.

The evening before Ryan's graduation from the program, Brice shared his story with the group. On his honeymoon cruise to South America, he and his new wife Talia signed up for some excursions. On their third excursion the tour guide took them to visit a remote waterfall hidden in a cave. During the excursion they witnessed the beauty of the waterfall and took pictures after the long trek to get there. On their way out of the cave another tourist with a powerful flash on his camera took a photo in a dark corner that disturbed a colony of bats. Out of nowhere bats began to swarm in what seemed to be groups of thousands. Everyone began to run, shove and stampede. When they emerged from the cave the bats followed and Talia was so frightened that she ran the opposite way of the crowd and ran off of the cave's cliff, plummeting to her death. It was a freak accident. When her body was recovered all her limbs were broken and her skull was broken in pieces. "The hardest thing I ever had to do was call my father in law to tell him that his daughter that he trusted me with, was gone," Brice explained. Talia was his college sweetheart and they met at a party his fraternity was hosting. He described her as smart, spicy and full of life. After the funeral, he began drinking didn't stop for 7 years. Ryan was moved by Brice's ability to tell the story without crying. He longed for the day when he could speak about Bradley without shedding tears.The following morning Blake sat in the audience as Ryan graduated from the Blakemore House. He is still encouraged to sit in grief meetings twice per month or whenever he needed to talk. Brice would check on him once per week and was available to talk 24/7. Blake was also presented with a certificate for being a supportive spouse. The graduates represented people from every walk of life demonstrating that trauma is no respecter of persons. Pride was glued on the faces of their loved ones as some people had been in the program for years. Missing was the man whose daughter was kidnapped who had since been transferred to a mental health facility.

Ryan stood at the altar in a cream tuxedo accompanied by his best man, Ryan Jr. The smooth sounds of *Best Part* by H.E.R and Daniel Caesar played as the maid of honor; Rayne walked down the aisle. Wearing a chocolate tulle skirt and matching sleeveless turtleneck, she waved and smiled at the seated guests. Smiling and skipping down the aisle was the ring bearer Royce who straightened up his act when he saw Ryan's face. Once Royce reached his spot on the platform a gold runner was rolled down the aisle and Brielle tossed orange petals along the way. Pastor Kemp asked everyone to stand to receive the bride

and the children's symphony began to play. Walking down the
aisle came Blake wearing a burnt orange trumpet dress with
sheer stomach and back panels. The bustline of the dress was
adorned in tone on tone crystals resembling a strapless
brassiere. With smoky eye makeup and a deep chocolate lip,
Blake killed, with her signature bob streaked with gold and
caramel highlights. She carried an orange and chocolate
bouquet adorned with crystals and feathers. Smiling at Ryan as
if he were the only person in the garden, the scent of *Soleil
Neige*, trailed behind her. When she arrived on the platform
Ryan whispered in her ear which made her giggle. Jason
welcomed the guests in attendance and proceeded with the
ceremony. After speaking specifically about Ryan and Blake's
love he directed everyone's attention to the screens on the sides
of the platform. When the video began, couples from GLC
spoke about how their marriages were strengthened or saved
by Blake and Ryan. As it continued colleagues in ministry testified how Blake and Ryan counseled them through rough times
and their business never came back to them through the
church grapevine. Words like integrity, sincerity and loyalty
were a common theme among the tributes. The video transi-
tioned to the family who expressed their admiration of Blake
and Ryan's union. Included in the tribute were Blake's step-
brothers and their wives which made her tear up. They needed
to get together soon. Another tearjerker came when Davina
and Nya thanked Blake for taking care of them. Lastly, Jason
interviewed the children and asked them what's the best part
about their parents. Rayne said they take care of her and love
her very much. Ryan Jr. said they give him money for new
games and Royce said they make good food. The video ended
with a clip of Bradley at 12 years old telling Blake she was the
best mom in the whole wide world, "I love you mom," said
Bradley while eerily waving goodbye. Ryan knew Blake needed
that after being called by her first name until his death. Blake

wiped her eyes with the hankie hidden in her hand. Jason moved the ceremony forward with the exchange of vows and rings. Ryan turned to Gavin in the crowd who was holding Tristan and brought him up to Ryan so he could untie the rings from his wrist. Everyone thought it was a precious surprise but Ryan didn't trust his best man or ring bearer with the rings. Always the responsible one, Rayne handed Ryan's ring to her mother. The couple chose to exchange Cartier love rings to have an alternative to their expensive diamond bands. Their vows meant so much more at year 15 than they could've ever meant at day one. They walked their vows out daily. Sometimes one more than the other but they began their journey as youngsters but vowed to continue their journey as a grown man and woman. Gavin and Victoria chose to walk away but Blake and Ryan had so many examples of couples willing to keep going. Jason finished the ceremony and announced them as "the grown and sexy Ryan and Blake Hairston." During the procession, the children ran up the aisle and Ryan grabbed Tristin on their way to the house to change. Everyone invited found their tables in the tents and the orchestra continued to play. In addition to serving as officiant, Jason was tasked with singing for the first dance. Kenneth sat at the table with Gavin, Victoria, Barbara, and Tia. The waiters brought around Hors'deouvres as the couple changed and took pictures. Royce, Rayne, and Ryan Jr. were already in the tent dancing. Ryan and Blake had a sweetheart table instead of a head table so the children could have fun. Jason stepped onto the stage and people began yelling out titles to his secular songs. Devin especially was one of his biggest fans. Gavin went outside to get Tristin back from Ryan so they could be announced. The orchestra began to play the strings to their first dance and Jason announced, "Once again let's give it up for the grown and sexy Ryan and Blake Hairston!" in a Randy Watson tone. Everyone stood and clapped as the couple walked to the dancefloor. Ryan changed into a classic black tux with gold tie and hankie and Blake wore a gold backless slip dress with orange, gold, and chocolate heels. The song melodiously made its way back to the beginning and Jason was ready to sing Don't Change by Musiq Soulchild. Ryan held his beautiful bride close as their guests looked on smiling and recording video. Blake looked over Ryan's face and loved how well he aged. His smooth chocolate skin was accented by the grey hairs in his beard. His eyes lovingly locked with hers with a deep abiding love that only time and trials create. Ryan sang along with Jason *"Don't you know, you'll always be the most beautiful woman I know. So, let me reassure you, darling that my feelings are truly unconditional."* Everyone began singing along with the chorus and swayed back and forth. Ryan sang his favorite part *"I was meant for you and you were meant for me, yeah and I'll make sure that I'll be everything you need, yeah. Girl the way we are is how it's gonna be just as long as your love don't change."* When the couple walked to their table to eat Jason asked Ryan and Blake if he could sing some songs for Devin during dance time and they agreed. The couple kept it simple and offered two choices. Purposely not inviting anyone with dietary restrictions and special needs they offered steak and lobster or crab cakes and shrimp. Ryan literally didn't invite Taylor Vance because they weren't offering vegan options. Taylor was the food police who annoyingly elected himself to govern your food choices and Ryan wasn't down for the foolery. Blake also didn't invite Rhoda's good friend Tabby because she was allergic to shellfish. Their no-nonsense approach had come after years of bending over backwards for people who wouldn't do the same. After dinner Ryan and Blake presented their tribute to Rhoda. So grateful and moved to tears for being appreciated, she told Blake and Ryan she'd do it again and again. The couple also gave their gifts to Joshua, Bella, Paris and Lexi which were couple's massages, dinner and smaller plaques. Blake danced with Kenneth, Evans and Gavin and Ryan danced with Victoria and Rhoda. Uncle Alex wearing an orange tuxedo, performed his famous shuffle. Vivian looked on cheering and Lexi was humiliated as always. Grandpa Rhodes and Mumzie showed up late citing the loving was too good to stop. Rhoda and Vivian shook their heads while Gavin and Pat were humiliated. Rhoda decided to bring the children in the house and prepare them for bed. Bella also prepared the children for bed and Brielle stayed in Rayne's room and Joshua Jr. stayed in Ryan Jr.'s room. Rhoda laid in Royce's room until he fell asleep. The moment Devin had been waiting for his whole life came to pass when Jason performed: *In the Shower, Let Me Love You* and *Grip It*. Though he was there in the crowd in Chicago it was nothing like a private performance. He sang the words to Zoe "Feel my rain in the shower, Feel my rain in the shower." Everyone had to admit, Jason had hits! While dancing Ryan expressed to Blake that he was used to having 4 kids. Blake teased him saying he had 4 because he was a grandfather. Ryan reminded her that people who make love after Jason sings his songs, always get pregnant. Blake kissed her beautiful king as he held her tight. Ryan whispered in Blake's ear "I can already see my baby girl Rylie Raquel Hairston."